JUST BEYOND™

VOLUME 8: TRAPPED FOREVER

Written by
R.L. Stine

Illustrated by
Kelly & Nichole Matthews

Lettered by
Mike Fiorentino

Cover by
Miguel Mercado

Just Beyond created by
R.L. Stine

Designer
Scott Newman

Assistant Editor
Michael Moccio

Associate Editor
Sophie Philips-Roberts

Editor
Bryce Carlson

ABDOBOOKS.COM

Reinforced library bound edition published in 2021 by Spotlight, a division of ABDO, PO Box 398166, Minneapolis, Minnesota 55439. Spotlight produces high-quality reinforced library bound editions for schools and libraries. Published by agreement with KaBOOM!

Printed in the United States of America, North Mankato, Minnesota.
092020 012021

kaboom!™

BOOM! Studios, 5670 Wilshire Boulevard, Suite 400, Los Angeles, CA 90036-5679.

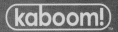

Library of Congress Control Number: 2020940822

THIS BOOK CONTAINS RECYCLED MATERIALS

Publisher's Cataloging-in-Publication Data

Names: Stine, R.L., author. | Matthews, Kelly; Matthews, Nichole, illustrators.
Title: Trapped forever / by R.L. Stine; illustrated by Kelly Matthews, and Nichole Matthews.
Description: Minneapolis, Minnesota : Spotlight, 2021. | Series: Just beyond; volume 8
Summary: Zammy and Juniper think driving to the forest will be their biggest hurdle in their latest attempt to get home, but after they arrive, they must capture a Martian bird to get their tracker back and avoid the kids trying to capture them.
Identifiers: ISBN 9781532147586 (lib. bdg.)
Subjects: LCSH: Camping--Juvenile fiction. | Families--Juvenile fiction. | Automobile driving--Juvenile fiction. | Birds--Juvenile fiction. | Extraterrestrial beings--Juvenile fiction. | Adventure stories--Juvenile fiction. | Graphic Novels--Juvenile fiction. | Comic books, strips, etc.--Juvenile fiction.
Classification: DDC 741.5--dc23

ABDO Spotlight

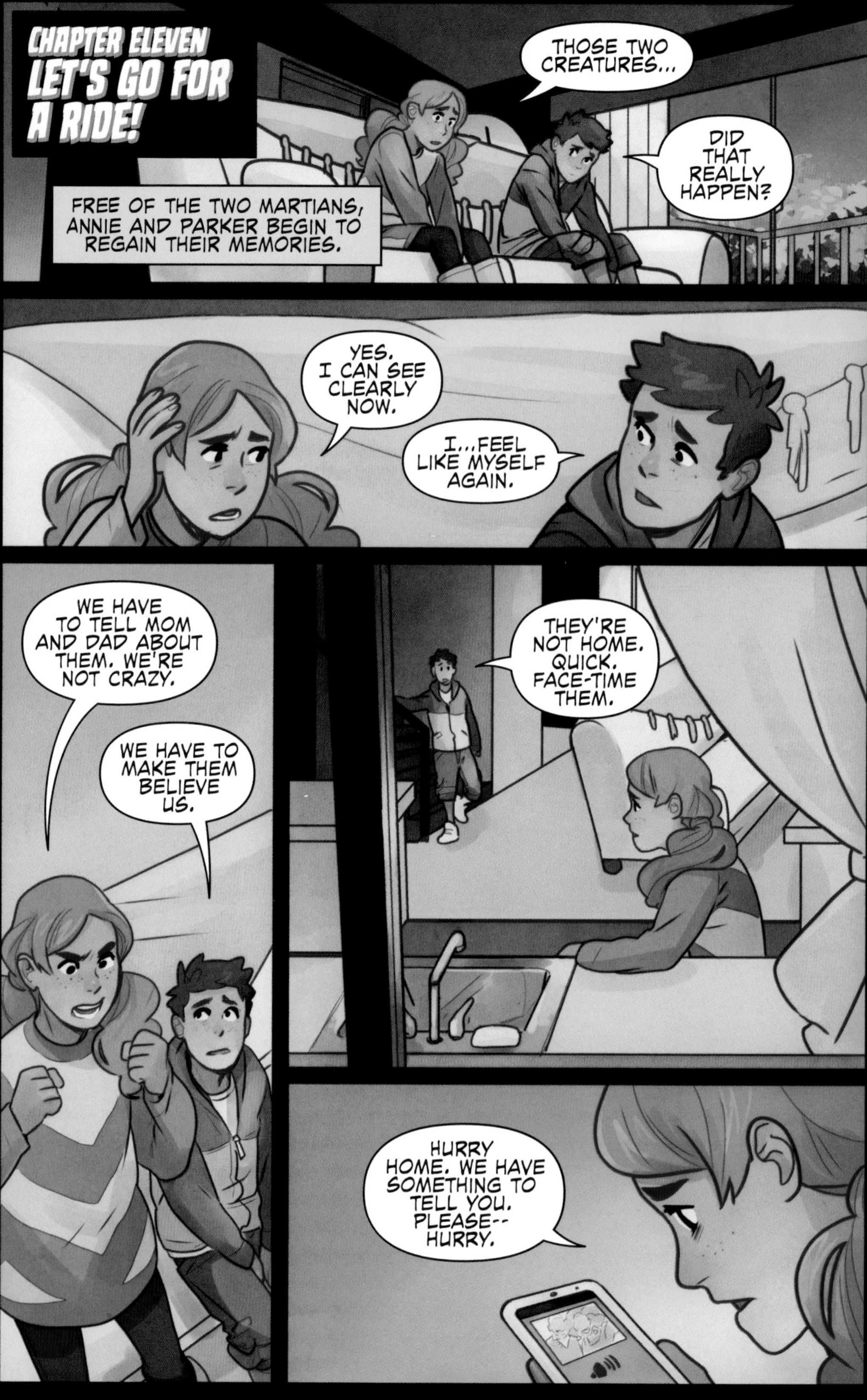
CHAPTER ELEVEN
LET'S GO FOR A RIDE!
THOSE TWO CREATURES...
DID THAT REALLY HAPPEN?
FREE OF THE TWO MARTIANS, ANNIE AND PARKER BEGIN TO REGAIN THEIR MEMORIES.
YES. I CAN SEE CLEARLY NOW.
I...FEEL LIKE MYSELF AGAIN.
WE HAVE TO TELL MOM AND DAD ABOUT THEM. WE'RE NOT CRAZY.
WE HAVE TO MAKE THEM BELIEVE US.
THEY'RE NOT HOME. QUICK. FACE-TIME THEM.
HURRY HOME. WE HAVE SOMETHING TO TELL YOU. PLEASE-- HURRY.

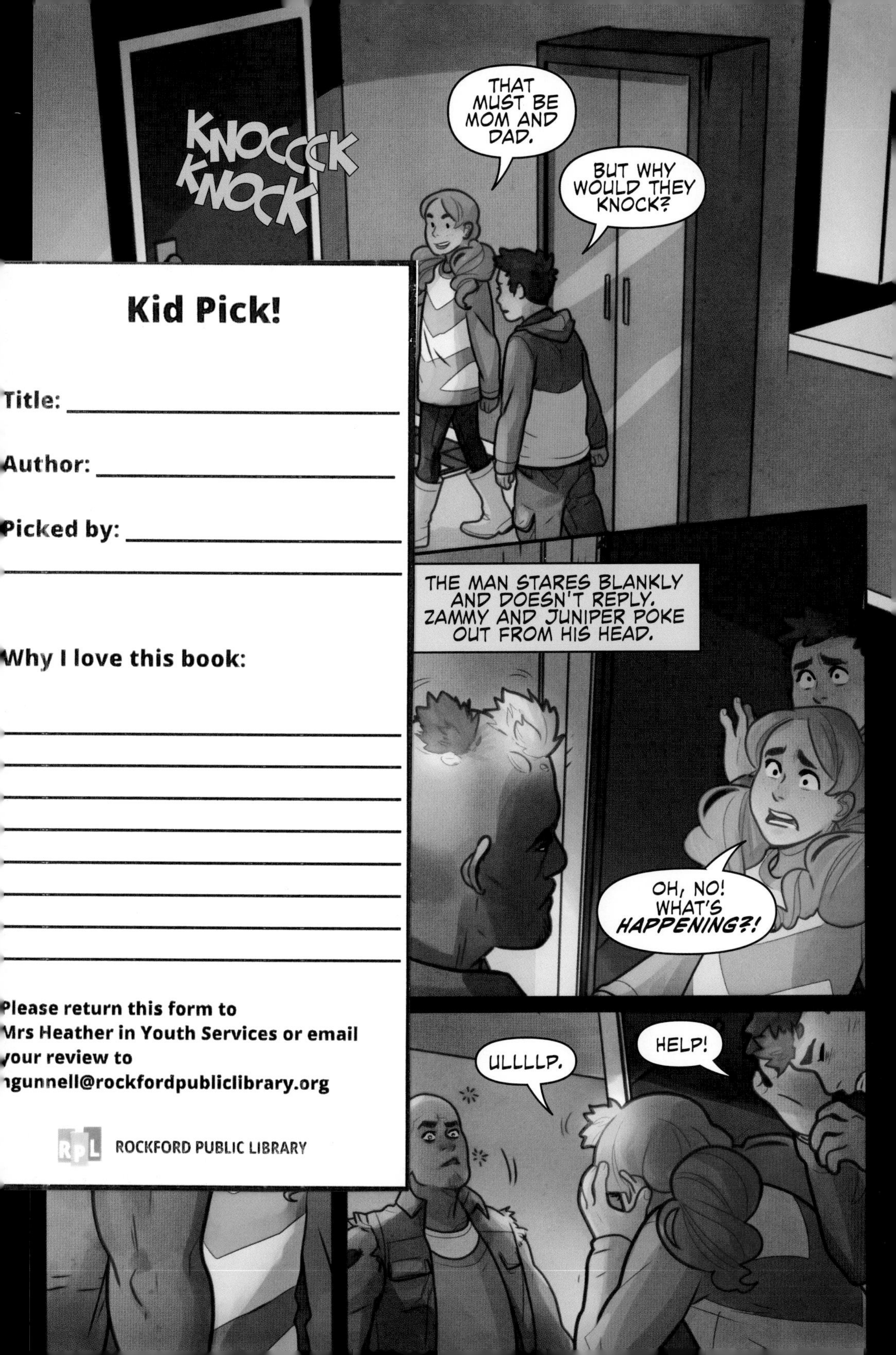
KNOCCCK KNOCK
THAT MUST BE MOM AND DAD.
BUT WHY WOULD THEY KNOCK?
THE MAN STARES BLANKLY AND DOESN'T REPLY. ZAMMY AND JUNIPER POKE OUT FROM HIS HEAD.
OH, NO! WHAT'S *HAPPENING?!*
ULLLLP.
HELP!

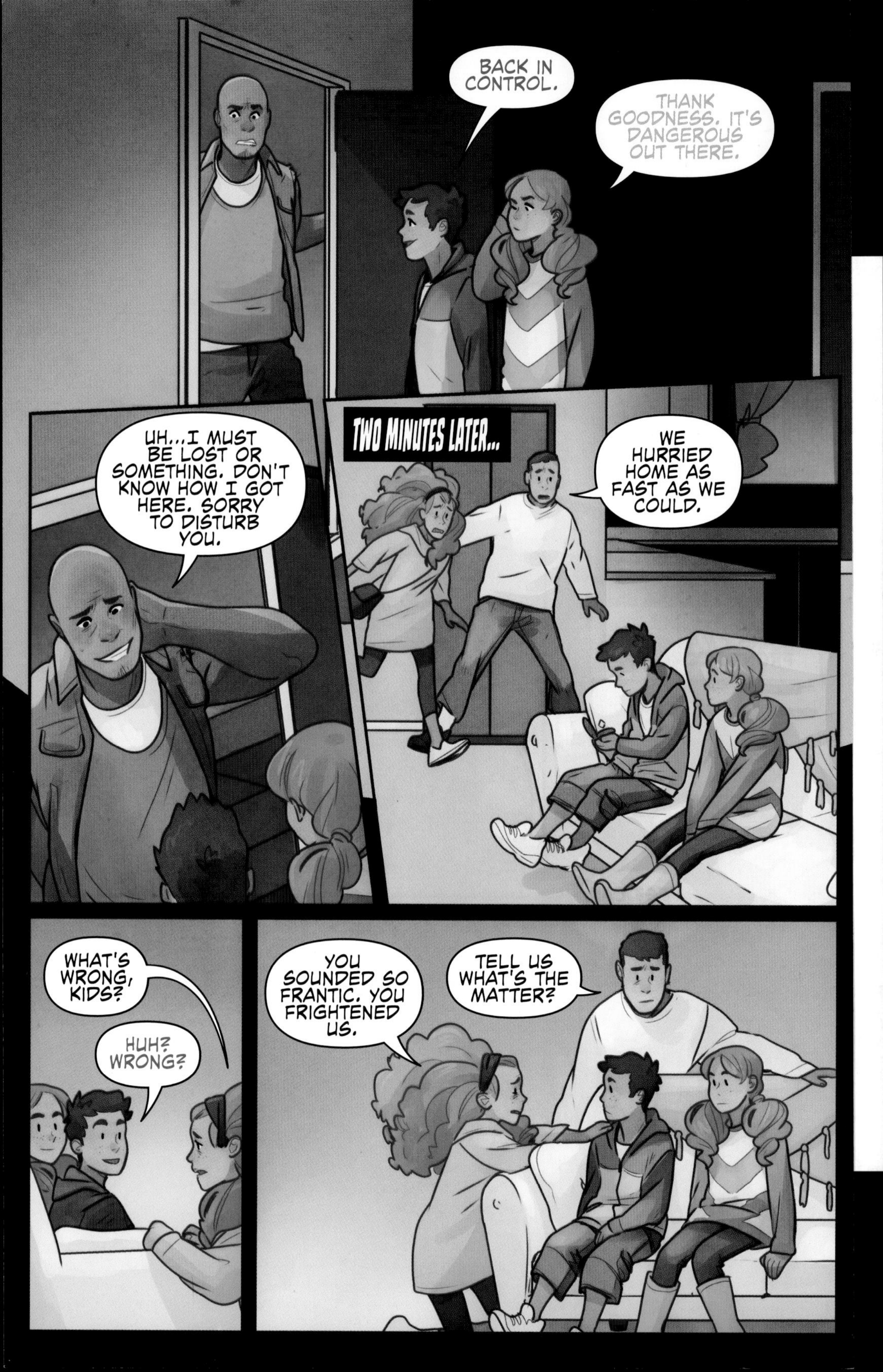
BACK IN CONTROL.
THANK GOODNESS. IT'S DANGEROUS OUT THERE.
UH...I MUST BE LOST OR SOMETHING. DON'T KNOW HOW I GOT HERE. SORRY TO DISTURB YOU.
TWO MINUTES LATER...
WE HURRIED HOME AS FAST AS WE COULD.
WHAT'S WRONG, KIDS?
HUH? WRONG?
YOU SOUNDED SO FRANTIC. YOU FRIGHTENED US.
TELL US WHAT'S THE MATTER?

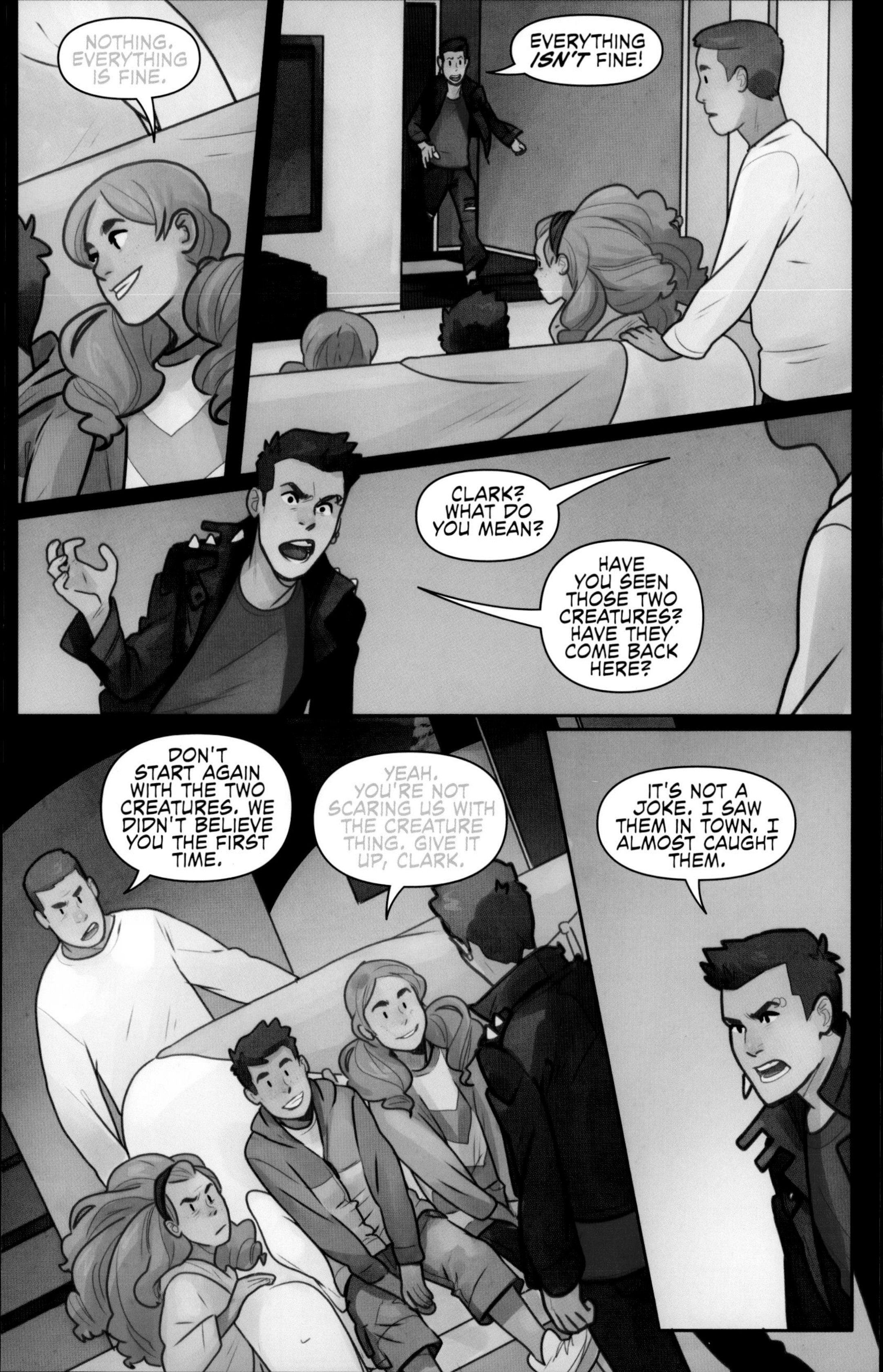
NOTHING. EVERYTHING IS FINE.
EVERYTHING *ISN'T* FINE!
CLARK? WHAT DO YOU MEAN?
HAVE YOU SEEN THOSE TWO CREATURES? HAVE THEY COME BACK HERE?
DON'T START AGAIN WITH THE TWO CREATURES. WE DIDN'T BELIEVE YOU THE FIRST TIME.
YEAH. YOU'RE NOT SCARING US WITH THE CREATURE THING. GIVE IT UP, CLARK.
IT'S NOT A JOKE. I SAW THEM IN TOWN. I ALMOST CAUGHT THEM.

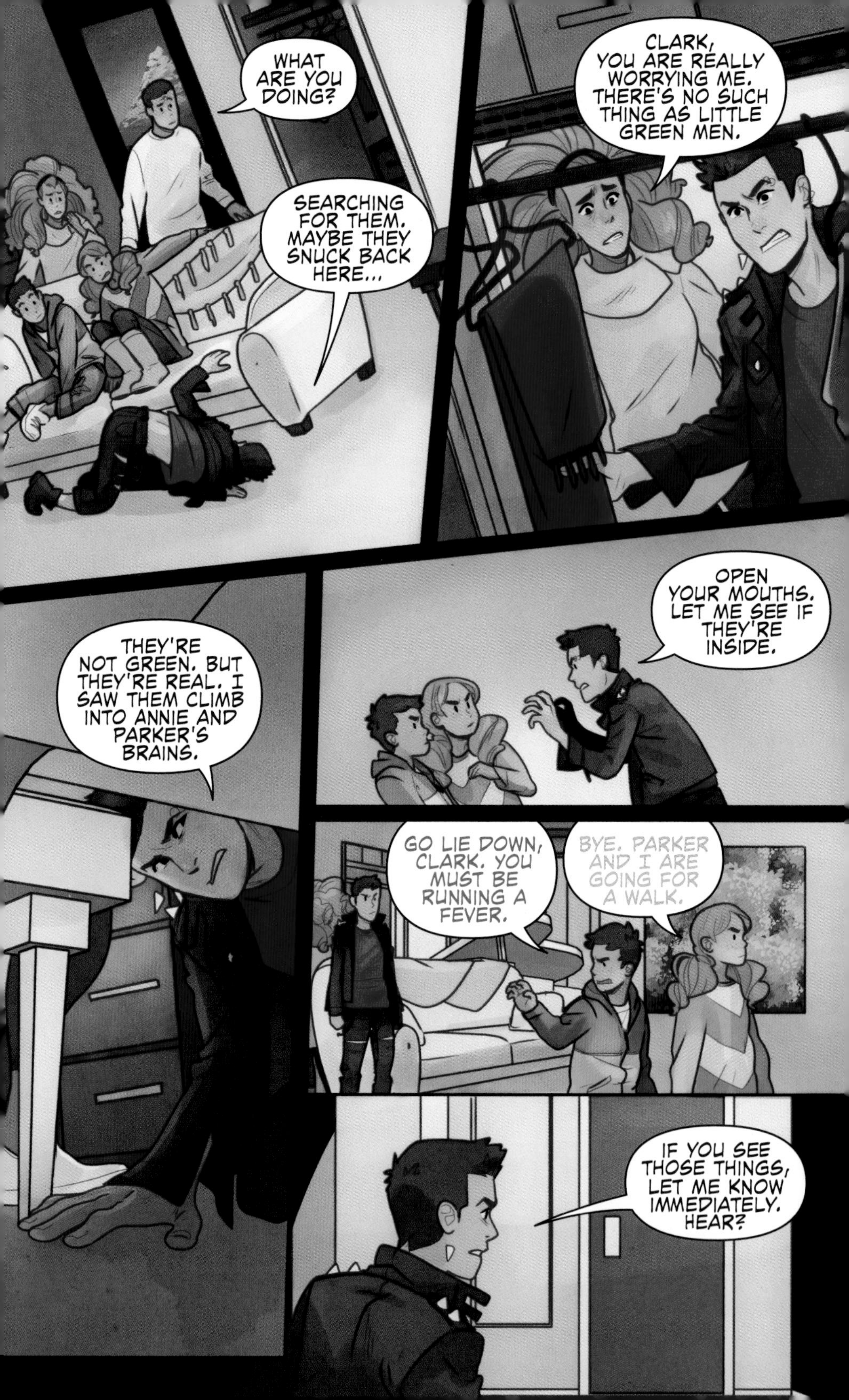
WHAT ARE YOU DOING?
SEARCHING FOR THEM. MAYBE THEY SNUCK BACK HERE...
CLARK, YOU ARE REALLY WORRYING ME. THERE'S NO SUCH THING AS LITTLE GREEN MEN.
THEY'RE NOT GREEN. BUT THEY'RE REAL. I SAW THEM CLIMB INTO ANNIE AND PARKER'S BRAINS.
OPEN YOUR MOUTHS. LET ME SEE IF THEY'RE INSIDE.
GO LIE DOWN, CLARK. YOU MUST BE RUNNING A FEVER.
BYE. PARKER AND I ARE GOING FOR A WALK.
IF YOU SEE THOSE THINGS, LET ME KNOW IMMEDIATELY. HEAR?

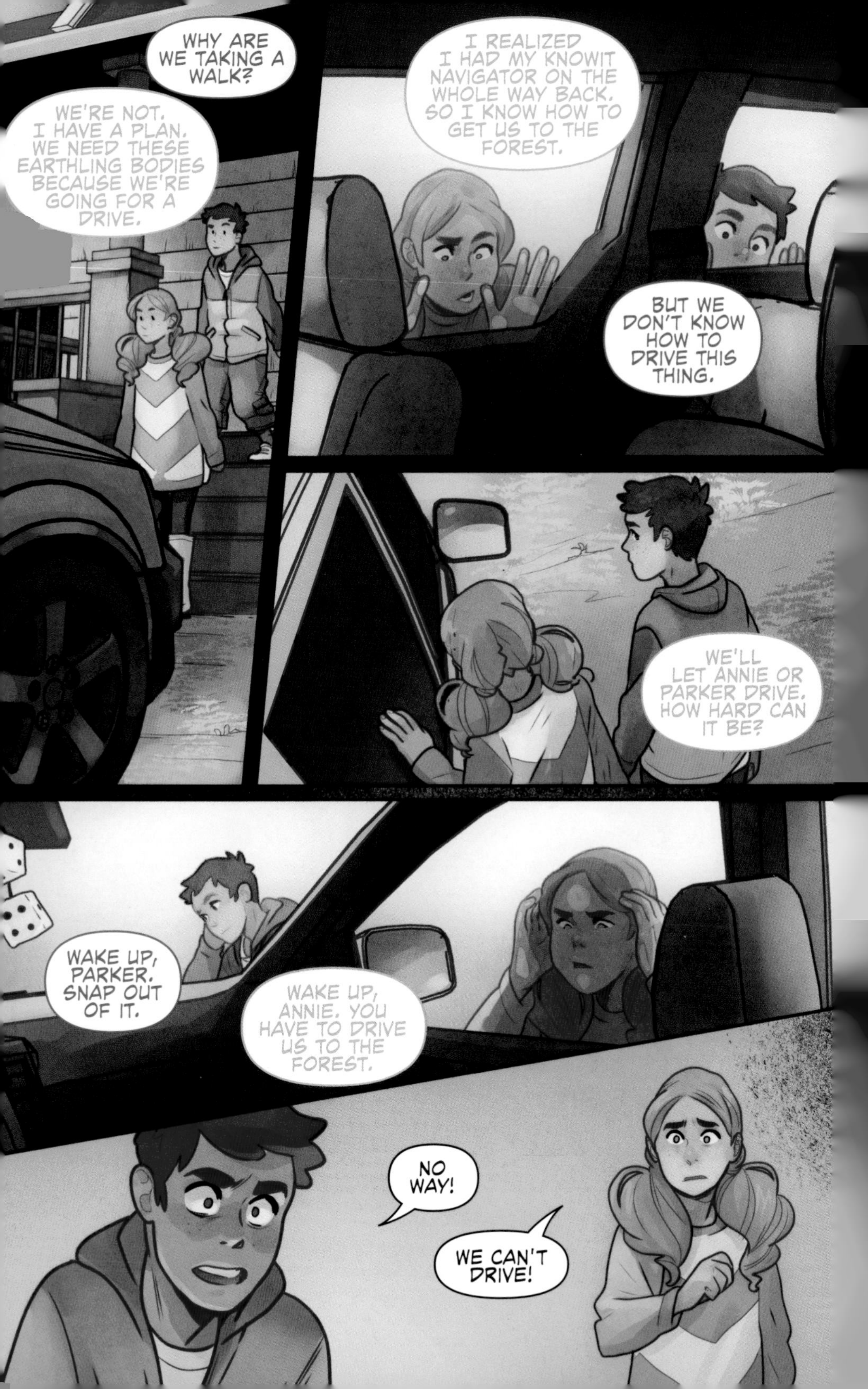
WHY ARE WE TAKING A WALK?
WE'RE NOT. I HAVE A PLAN. WE NEED THESE EARTHLING BODIES BECAUSE WE'RE GOING FOR A DRIVE.
I REALIZED I HAD MY KNOWIT NAVIGATOR ON THE WHOLE WAY BACK, SO I KNOW HOW TO GET US TO THE FOREST.
BUT WE DON'T KNOW HOW TO DRIVE THIS THING.
WE'LL LET ANNIE OR PARKER DRIVE. HOW HARD CAN IT BE?
WAKE UP, PARKER. SNAP OUT OF IT.
WAKE UP, ANNIE. YOU HAVE TO DRIVE US TO THE FOREST.
NO WAY!
WE CAN'T DRIVE!

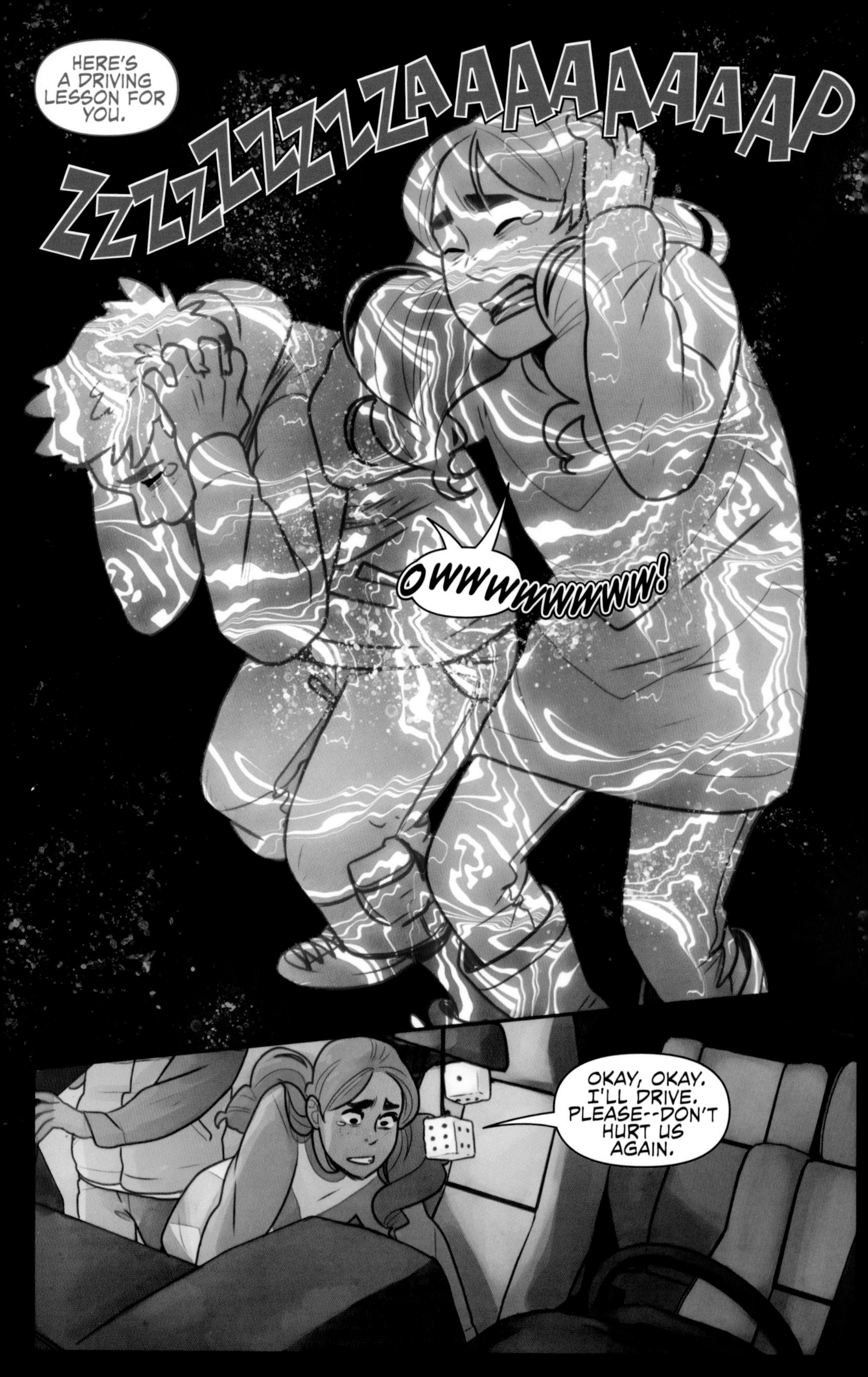
HERE'S A DRIVING LESSON FOR YOU.
ZZZZZZZZZAAAAAAAAAP
OWWWWWWWW!
OKAY, OKAY. I'LL DRIVE. PLEASE--DON'T HURT US AGAIN.

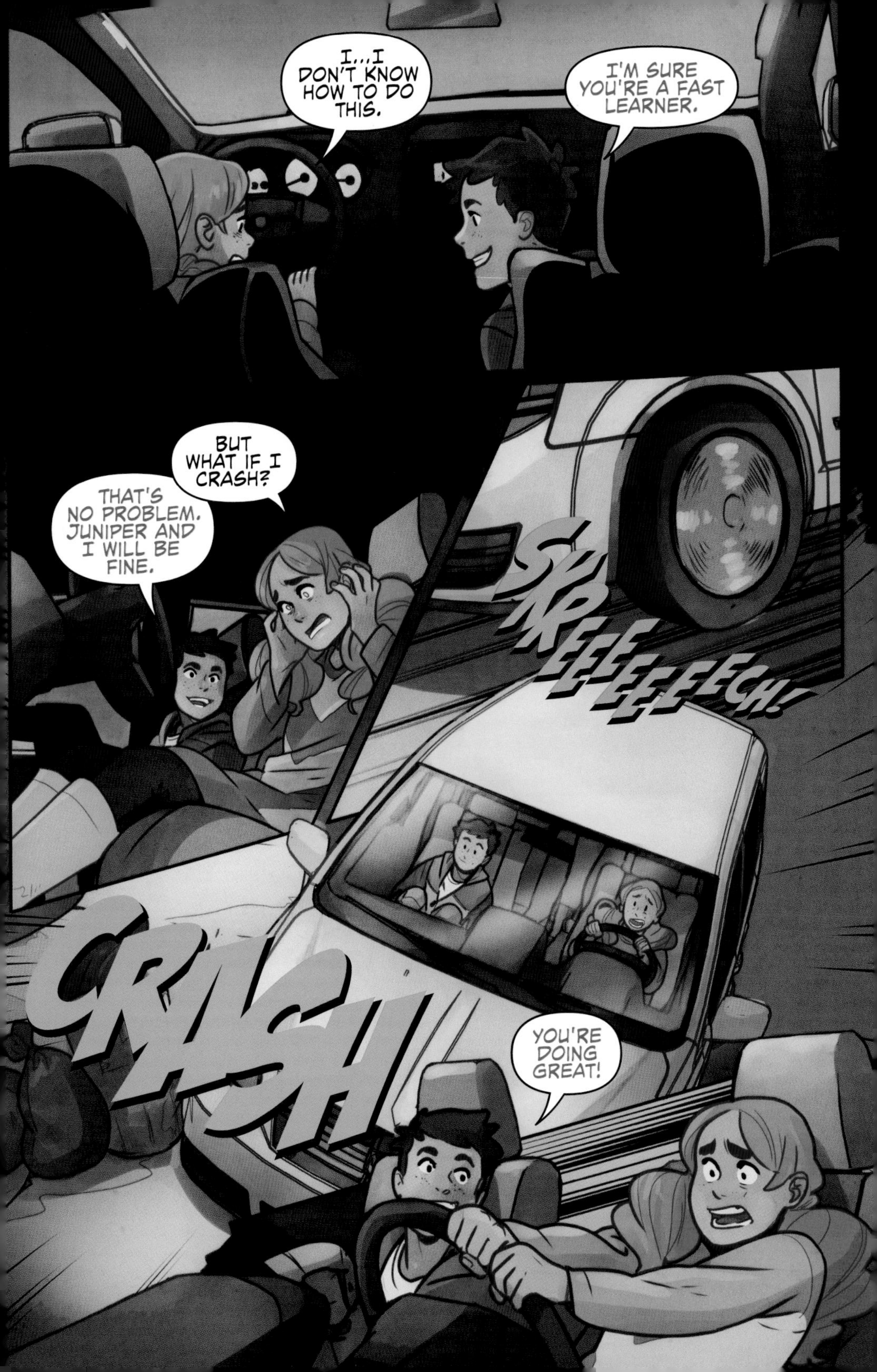
I...I DON'T KNOW HOW TO DO THIS.
I'M SURE YOU'RE A FAST LEARNER.
BUT WHAT IF I CRASH?
THAT'S NO PROBLEM. JUNIPER AND I WILL BE FINE.
SKREEEEEEECH!
CRASH
YOU'RE DOING GREAT!

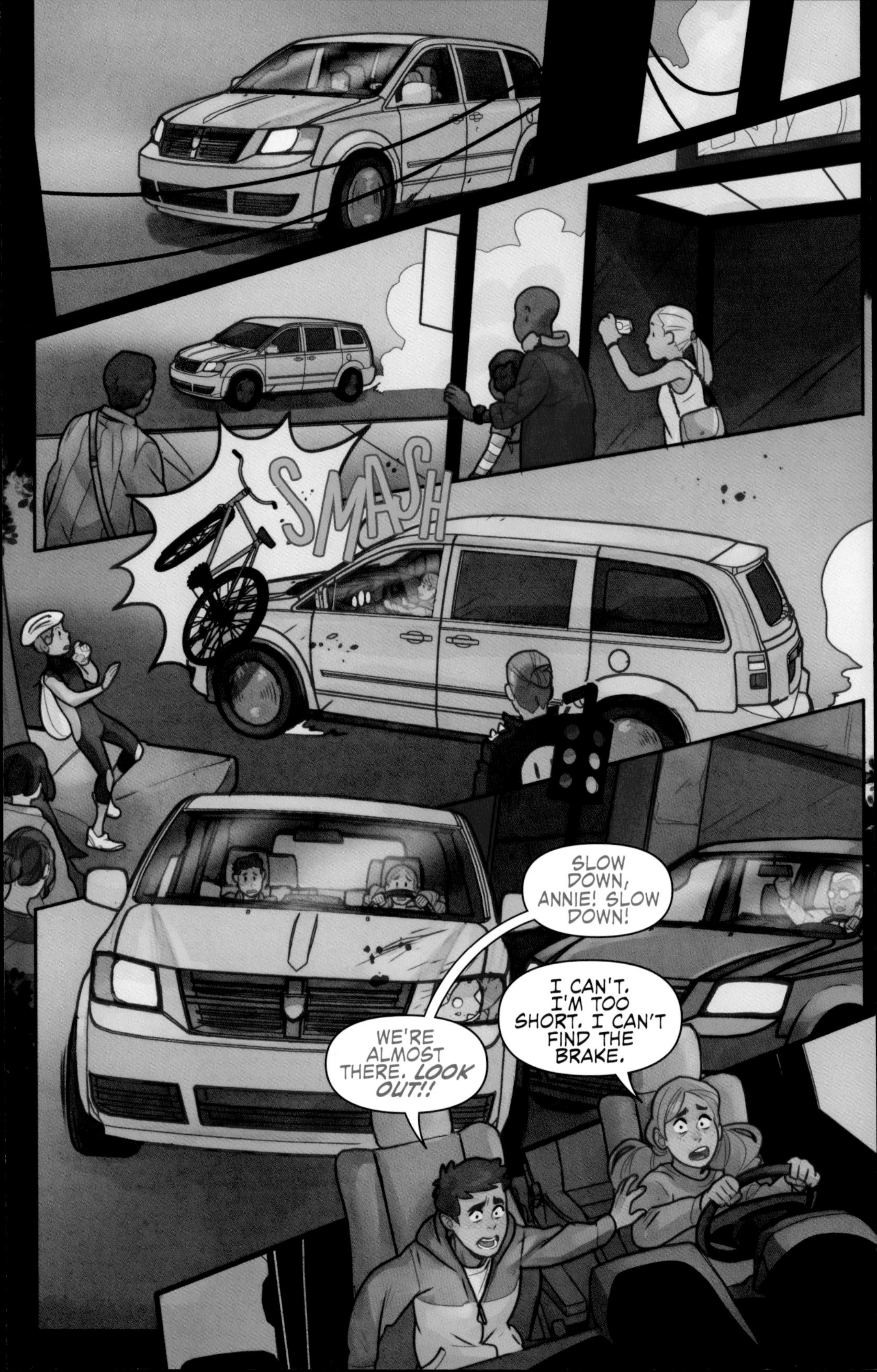
SMASH
SLOW DOWN, ANNIE! SLOW DOWN!
I CAN'T. I'M TOO SHORT. I CAN'T FIND THE BRAKE.
WE'RE ALMOST THERE. LOOK OUT!!

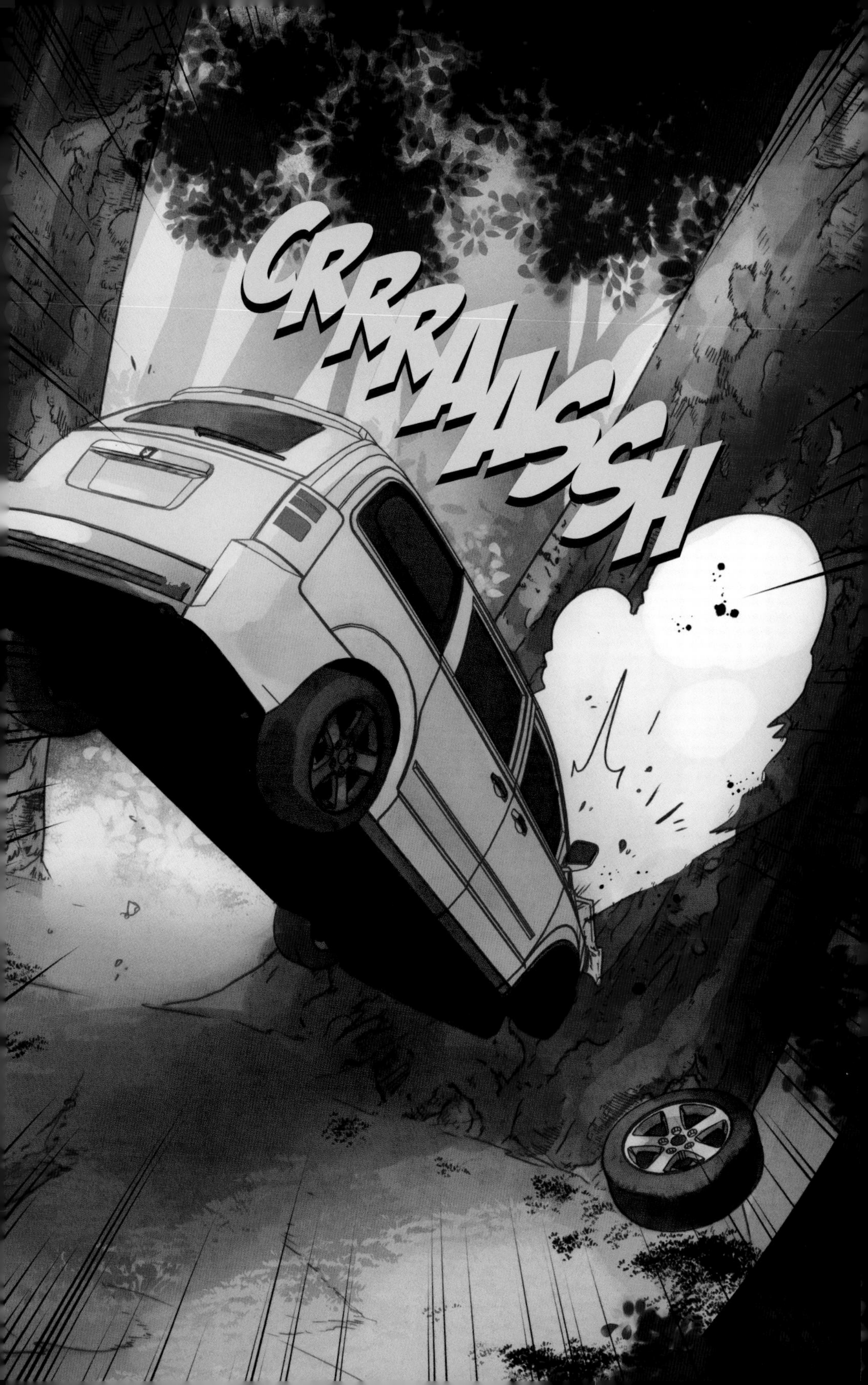
CRRRAASSH

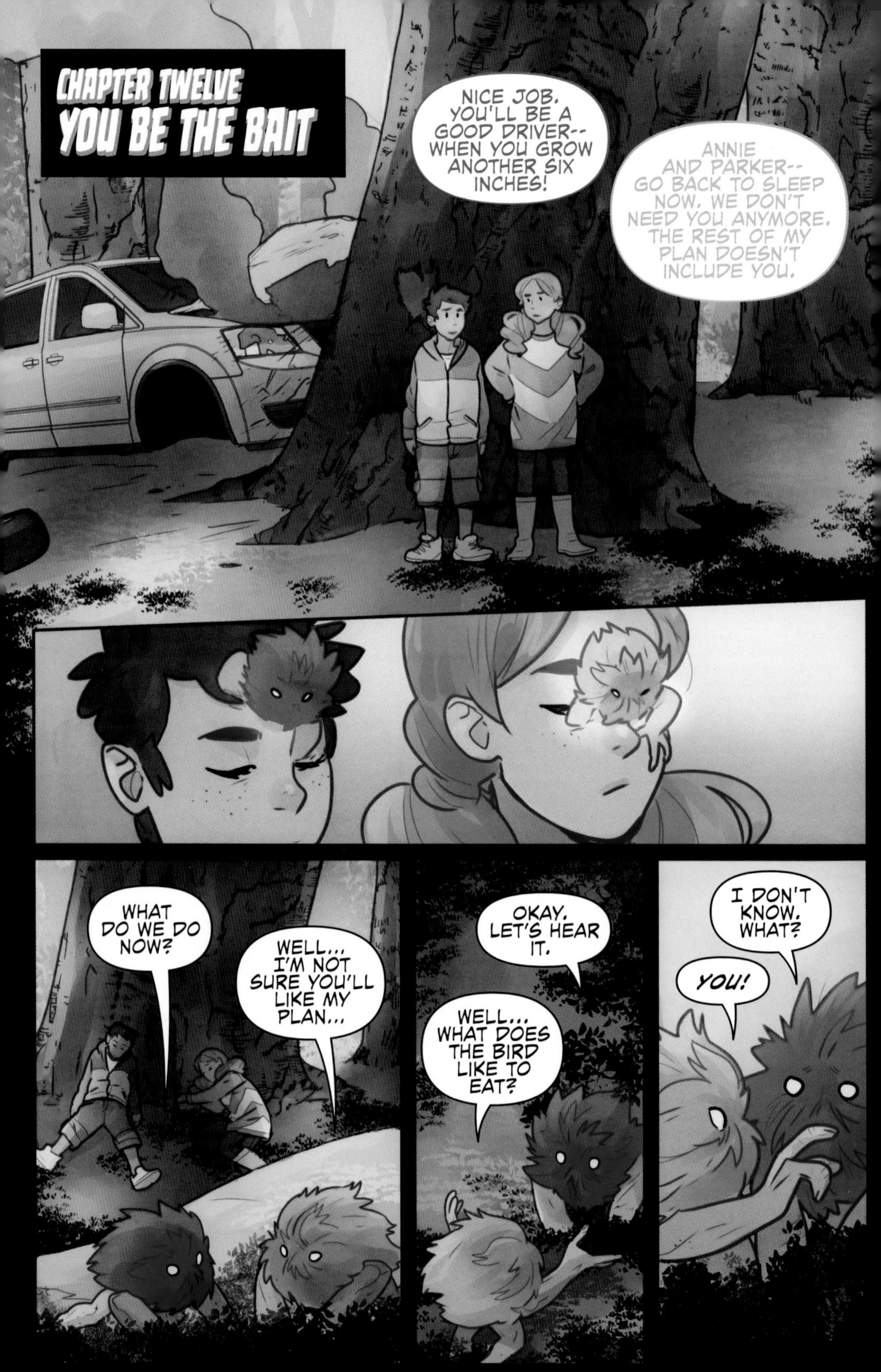
CHAPTER TWELVE
YOU BE THE BAIT
NICE JOB. YOU'LL BE A GOOD DRIVER-- WHEN YOU GROW ANOTHER SIX INCHES!
ANNIE AND PARKER-- GO BACK TO SLEEP NOW. WE DON'T NEED YOU ANYMORE. THE REST OF MY PLAN DOESN'T INCLUDE YOU.
WHAT DO WE DO NOW?
WELL... I'M NOT SURE YOU'LL LIKE MY PLAN...
OKAY. LET'S HEAR IT.
WELL... WHAT DOES THE BIRD LIKE TO EAT?
I DON'T KNOW. WHAT?
YOU!

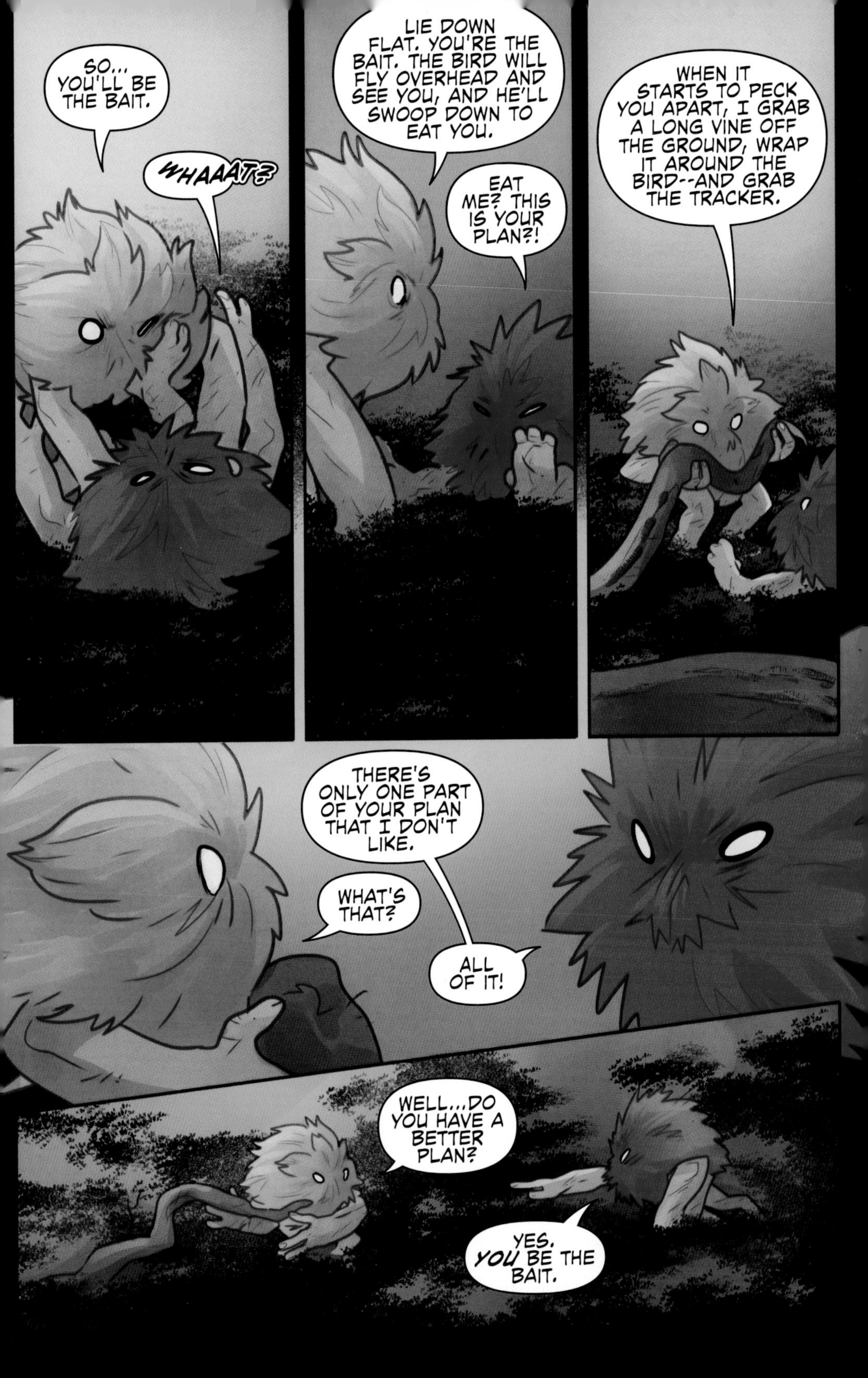
SO... YOU'LL BE THE BAIT.
WHAAAT?
LIE DOWN FLAT. YOU'RE THE BAIT. THE BIRD WILL FLY OVERHEAD AND SEE YOU, AND HE'LL SWOOP DOWN TO EAT YOU.
EAT ME? THIS IS YOUR PLAN?!
WHEN IT STARTS TO PECK YOU APART, I GRAB A LONG VINE OFF THE GROUND, WRAP IT AROUND THE BIRD--AND GRAB THE TRACKER.
THERE'S ONLY ONE PART OF YOUR PLAN THAT I DON'T LIKE.
WHAT'S THAT?
ALL OF IT!
WELL...DO YOU HAVE A BETTER PLAN?
YES. YOU BE THE BAIT.

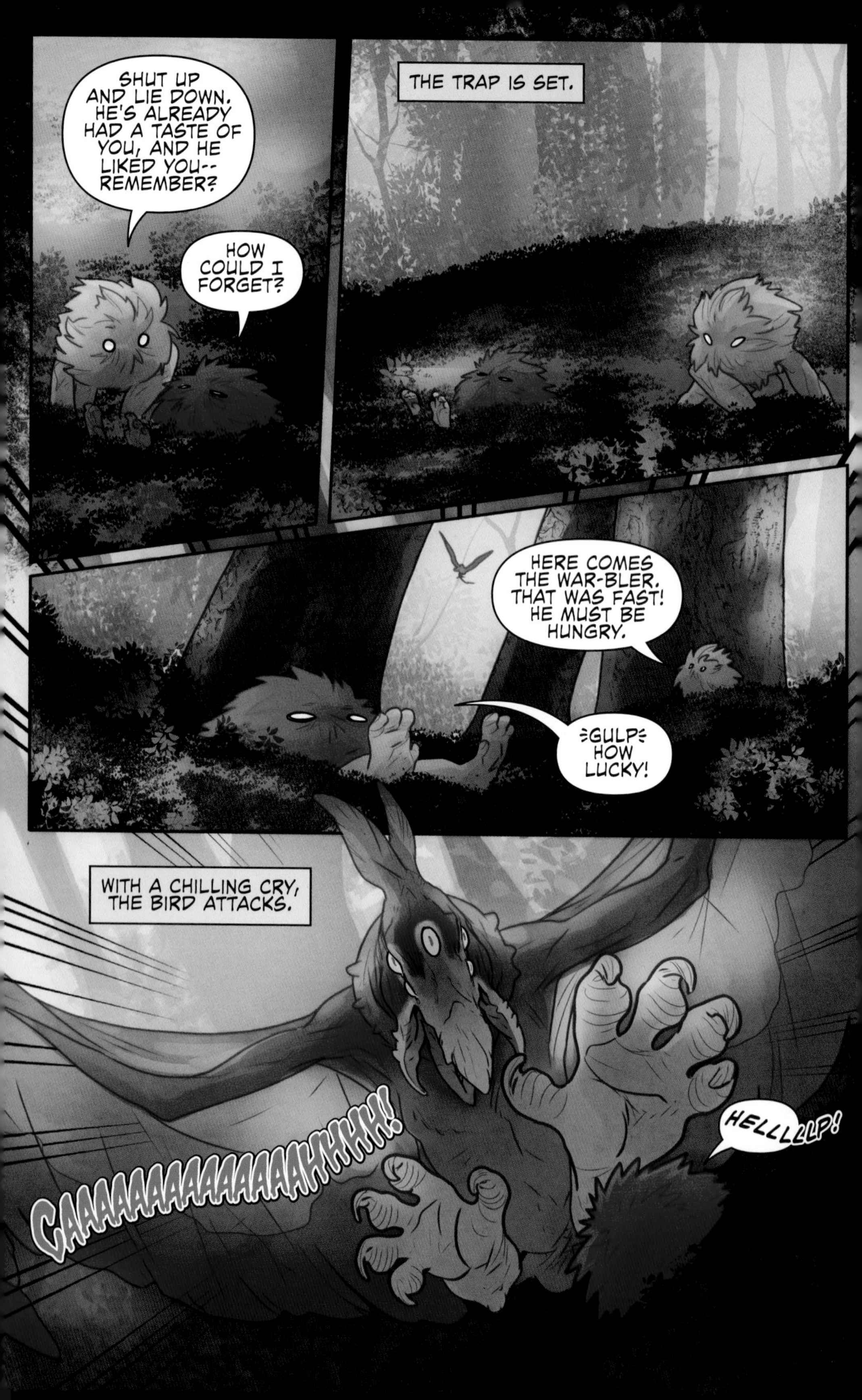
SHUT UP AND LIE DOWN. HE'S ALREADY HAD A TASTE OF YOU, AND HE LIKED YOU-- REMEMBER?
HOW COULD I FORGET?
THE TRAP IS SET.
HERE COMES THE WAR-BLER. THAT WAS FAST! HE MUST BE HUNGRY.
GULP HOW LUCKY!
WITH A CHILLING CRY, THE BIRD ATTACKS.
CAAAAAAAAAAAAAAHHHH!
HELLLLLP!

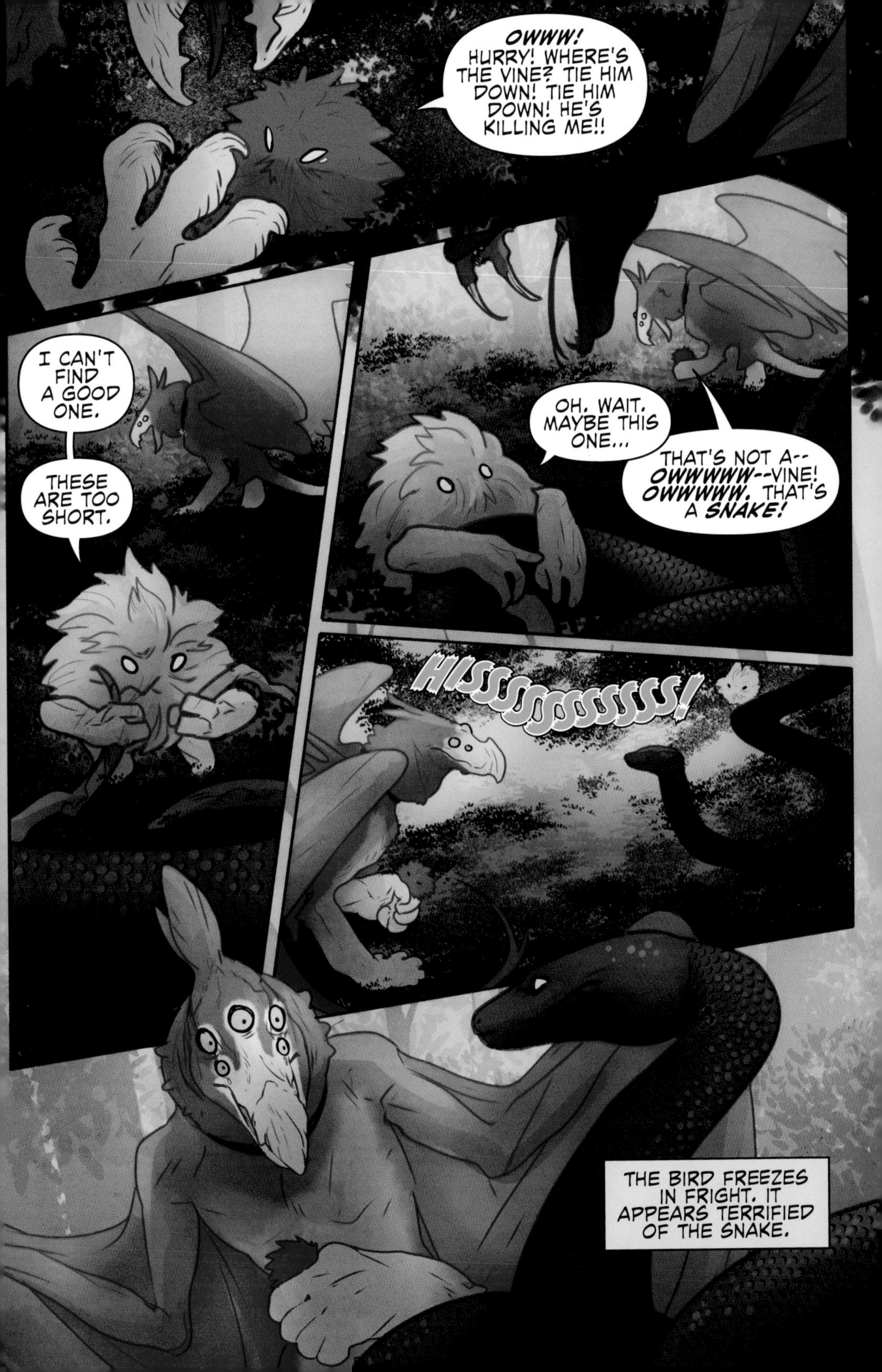
OWWW! HURRY! WHERE'S THE VINE? TIE HIM DOWN! TIE HIM DOWN! HE'S KILLING ME!!
I CAN'T FIND A GOOD ONE.
THESE ARE TOO SHORT.
OH. WAIT. MAYBE THIS ONE...
THAT'S NOT A-- OWWWWW--VINE! OWWWWW. THAT'S A SNAKE!
HISSSSSSSSSSSS!
THE BIRD FREEZES IN FRIGHT. IT APPEARS TERRIFIED OF THE SNAKE.

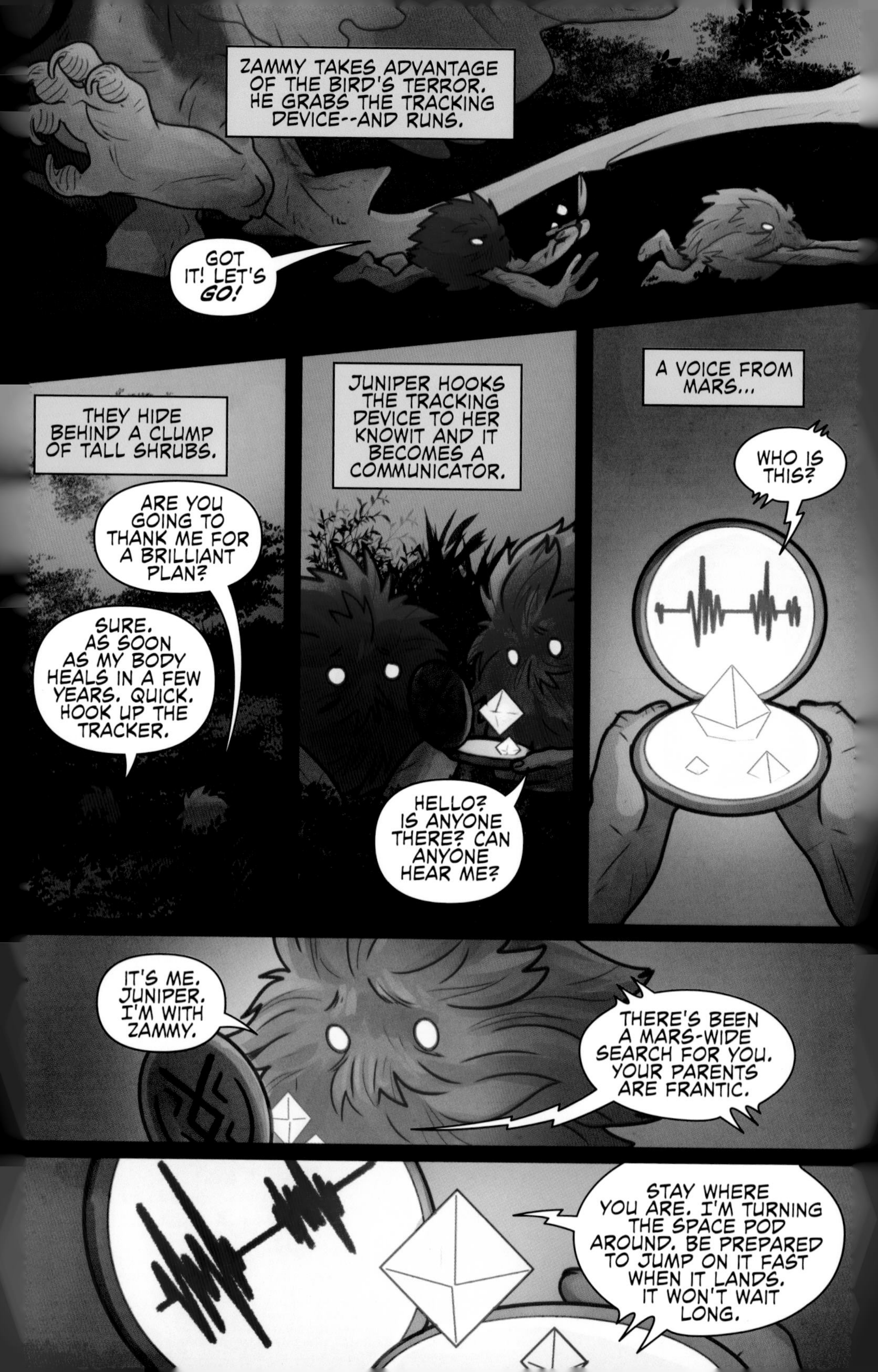
ZAMMY TAKES ADVANTAGE OF THE BIRD'S TERROR. HE GRABS THE TRACKING DEVICE--AND RUNS.
GOT IT! LET'S GO!
THEY HIDE BEHIND A CLUMP OF TALL SHRUBS.
ARE YOU GOING TO THANK ME FOR A BRILLIANT PLAN?
SURE. AS SOON AS MY BODY HEALS IN A FEW YEARS. QUICK. HOOK UP THE TRACKER.
JUNIPER HOOKS THE TRACKING DEVICE TO HER KNOWIT AND IT BECOMES A COMMUNICATOR.
HELLO? IS ANYONE THERE? CAN ANYONE HEAR ME?
A VOICE FROM MARS...
WHO IS THIS?
IT'S ME. JUNIPER. I'M WITH ZAMMY.
THERE'S BEEN A MARS-WIDE SEARCH FOR YOU. YOUR PARENTS ARE FRANTIC.
STAY WHERE YOU ARE. I'M TURNING THE SPACE POD AROUND. BE PREPARED TO JUMP ON IT FAST WHEN IT LANDS. IT WON'T WAIT LONG.

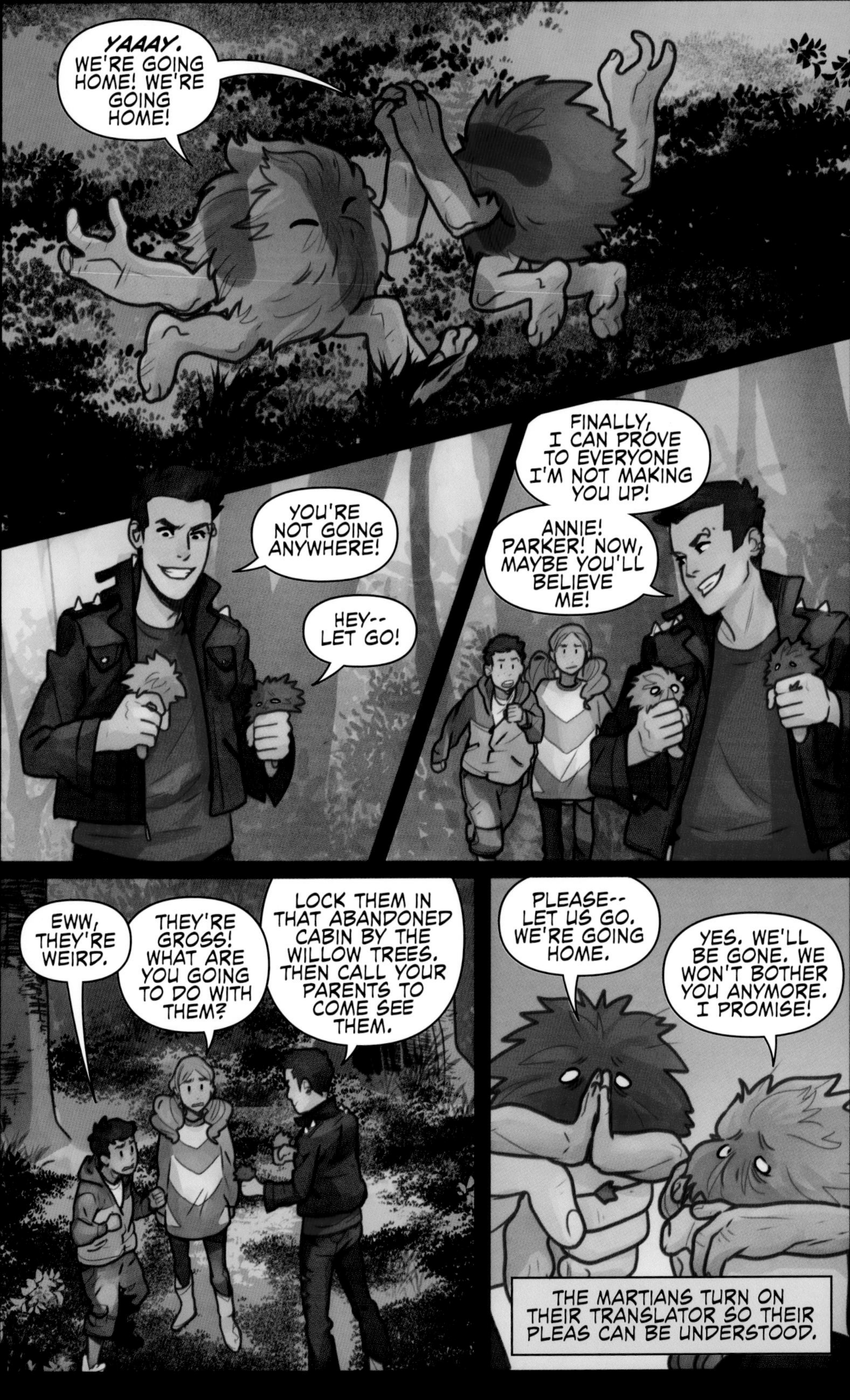
YAAAY. WE'RE GOING HOME! WE'RE GOING HOME!
YOU'RE NOT GOING ANYWHERE!
HEY-- LET GO!
FINALLY, I CAN PROVE TO EVERYONE I'M NOT MAKING YOU UP!
ANNIE! PARKER! NOW, MAYBE YOU'LL BELIEVE ME!
EWW, THEY'RE WEIRD.
THEY'RE GROSS! WHAT ARE YOU GOING TO DO WITH THEM?
LOCK THEM IN THAT ABANDONED CABIN BY THE WILLOW TREES. THEN CALL YOUR PARENTS TO COME SEE THEM.
PLEASE-- LET US GO. WE'RE GOING HOME.
YES. WE'LL BE GONE. WE WON'T BOTHER YOU ANYMORE. I PROMISE!
THE MARTIANS TURN ON THEIR TRANSLATOR SO THEIR PLEAS CAN BE UNDERSTOOD.

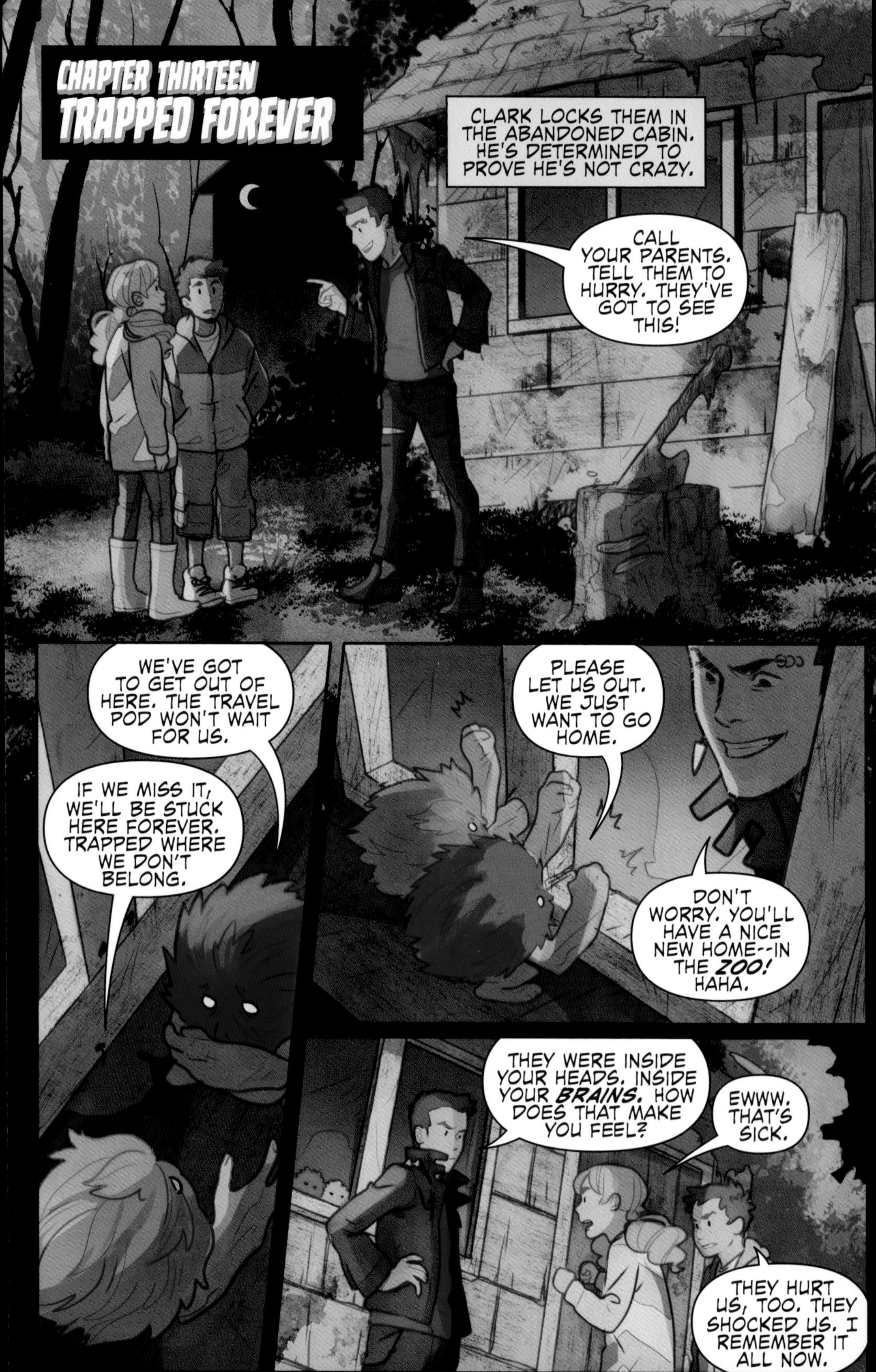
CHAPTER THIRTEEN
TRAPPED FOREVER
CLARK LOCKS THEM IN THE ABANDONED CABIN. HE'S DETERMINED TO PROVE HE'S NOT CRAZY.
CALL YOUR PARENTS. TELL THEM TO HURRY. THEY'VE GOT TO SEE THIS!
WE'VE GOT TO GET OUT OF HERE. THE TRAVEL POD WON'T WAIT FOR US.
IF WE MISS IT, WE'LL BE STUCK HERE FOREVER. TRAPPED WHERE WE DON'T BELONG.
PLEASE LET US OUT. WE JUST WANT TO GO HOME.
DON'T WORRY. YOU'LL HAVE A NICE NEW HOME--IN THE ZOO! HAHA.
THEY WERE INSIDE YOUR HEADS. INSIDE YOUR BRAINS. HOW DOES THAT MAKE YOU FEEL?
EWWW. THAT'S SICK.
THEY HURT US, TOO. THEY SHOCKED US. I REMEMBER IT ALL NOW.

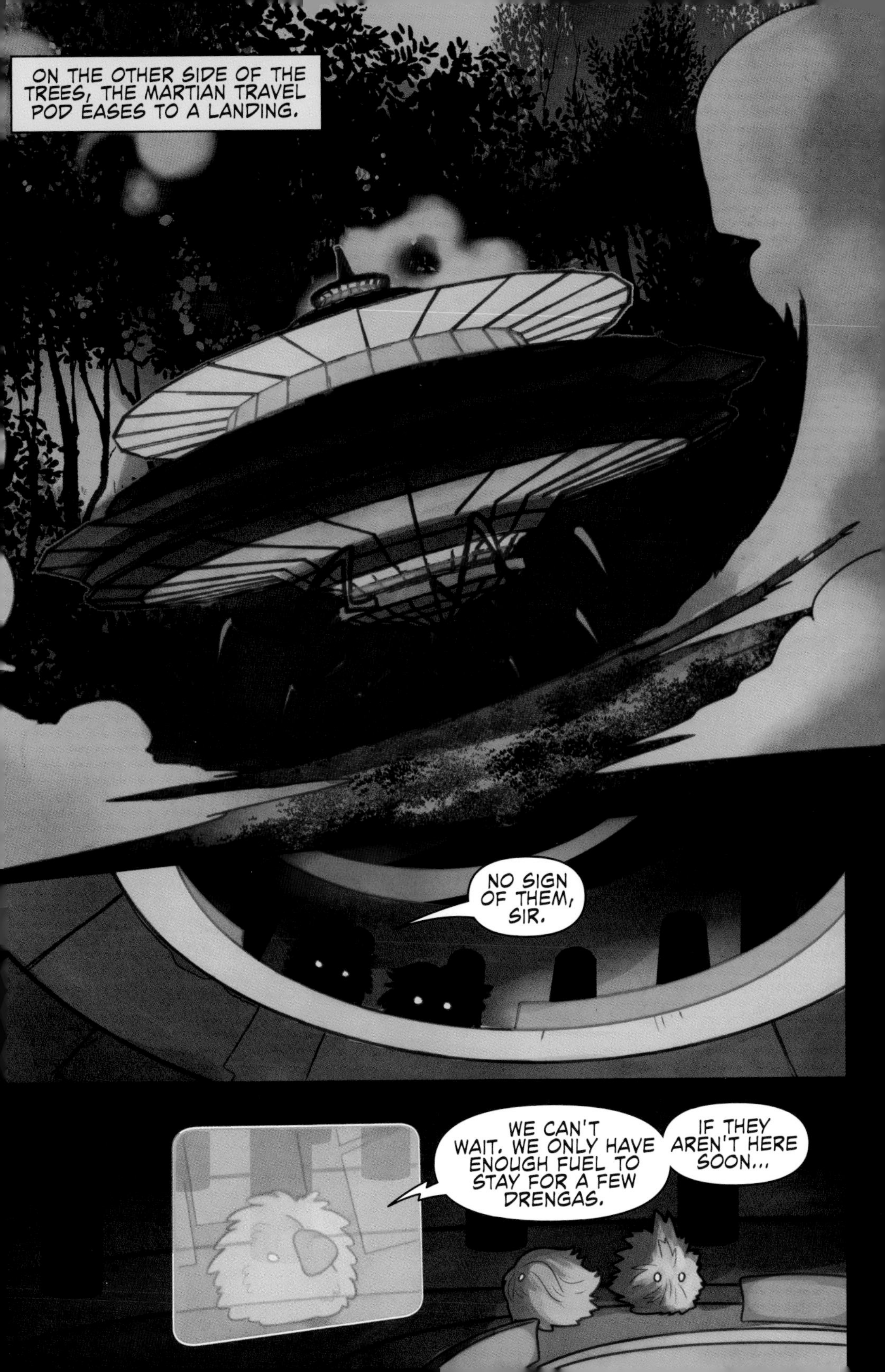
ON THE OTHER SIDE OF THE TREES, THE MARTIAN TRAVEL POD EASES TO A LANDING.
NO SIGN OF THEM, SIR.
WE CAN'T WAIT. WE ONLY HAVE ENOUGH FUEL TO STAY FOR A FEW DRENGAS.
IF THEY AREN'T HERE SOON...

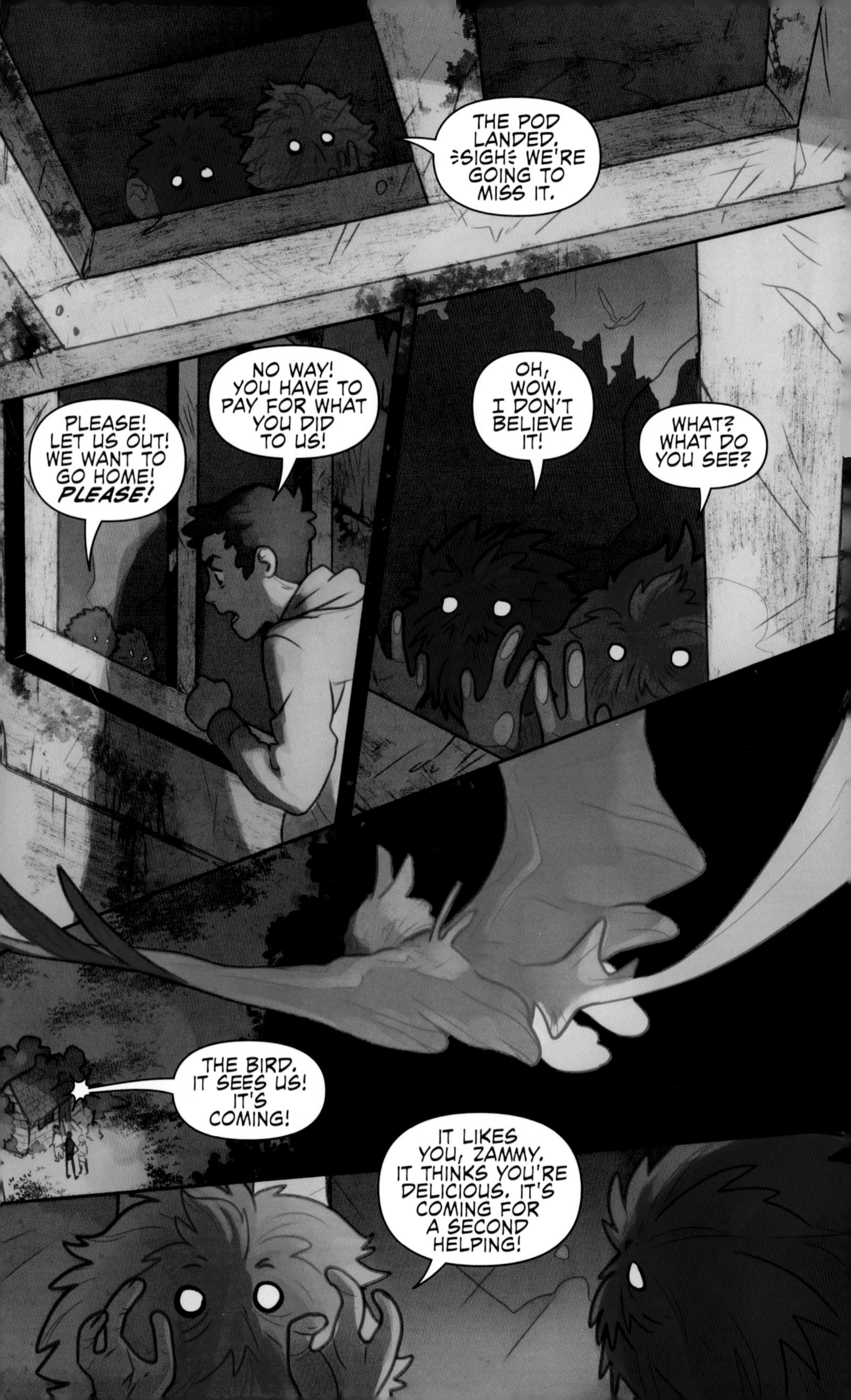
THE POD LANDED. ≤SIGH≥ WE'RE GOING TO MISS IT.
PLEASE! LET US OUT! WE WANT TO GO HOME! *PLEASE!*
NO WAY! YOU HAVE TO PAY FOR WHAT YOU DID TO US!
OH, WOW. I DON'T BELIEVE IT!
WHAT? WHAT DO YOU SEE?
THE BIRD. IT SEES US! IT'S COMING!
IT LIKES YOU, ZAMMY. IT THINKS YOU'RE DELICIOUS. IT'S COMING FOR A SECOND HELPING!

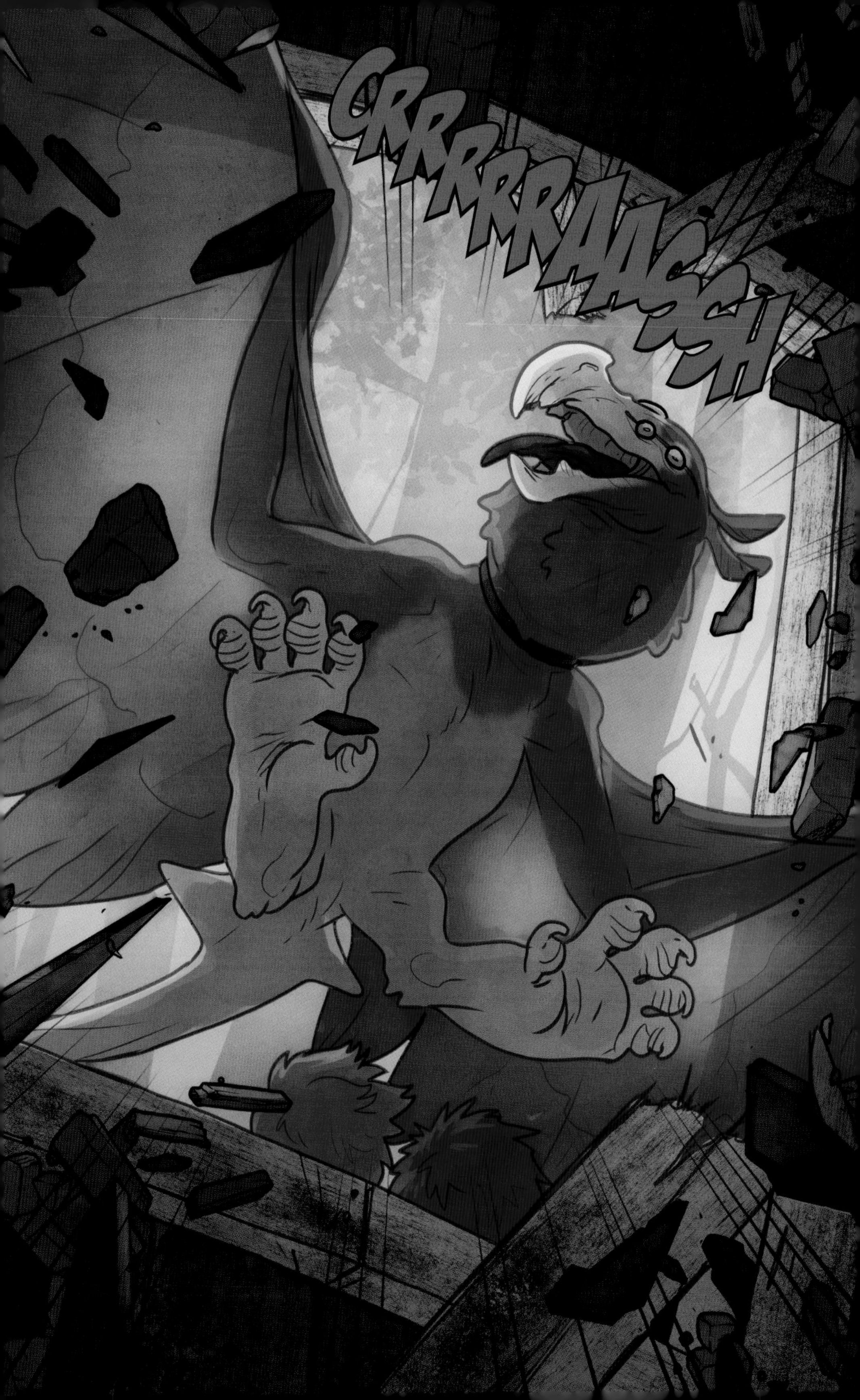
CRRRRAACSH

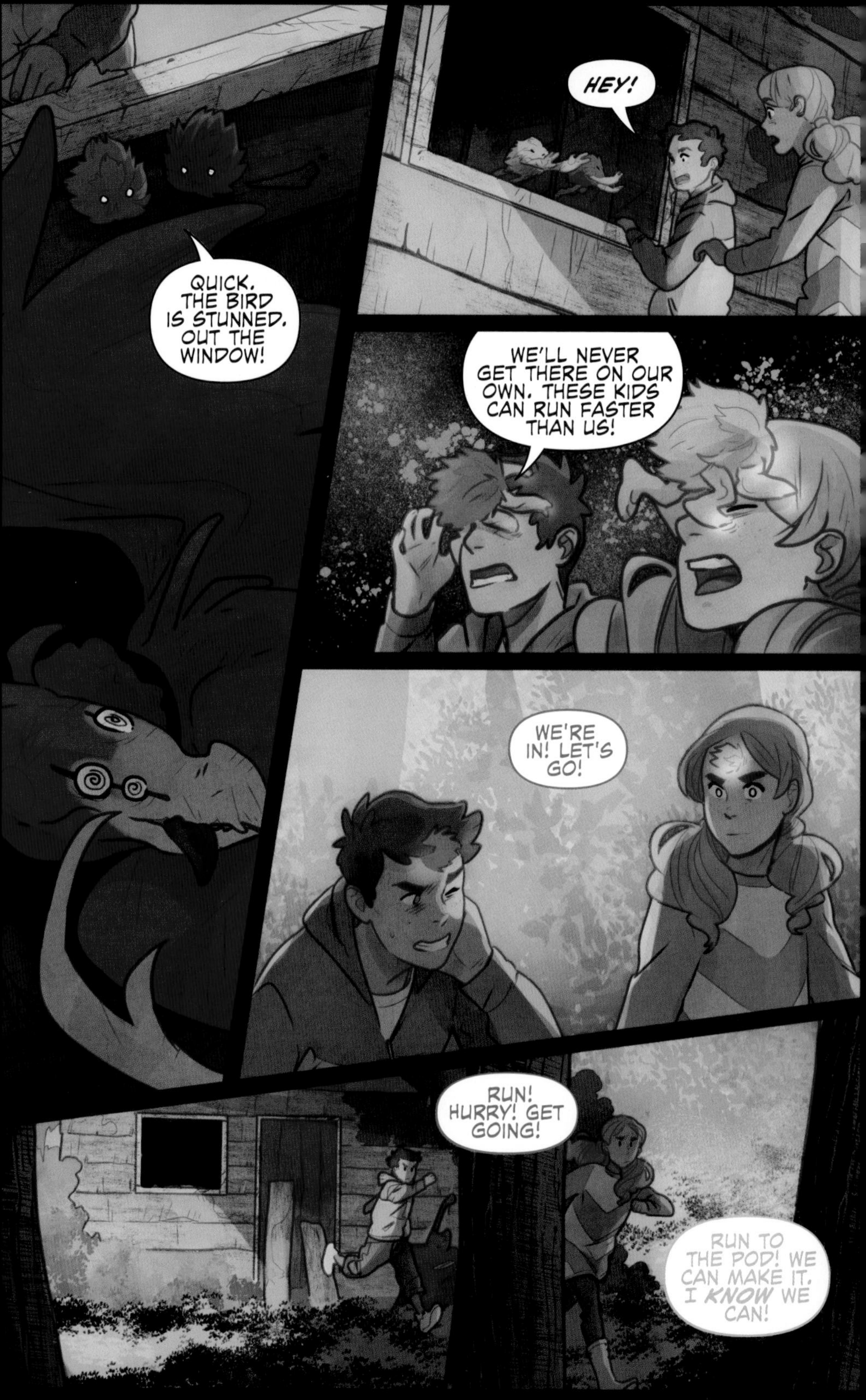
QUICK. THE BIRD IS STUNNED. OUT THE WINDOW!
HEY!
WE'LL NEVER GET THERE ON OUR OWN. THESE KIDS CAN RUN FASTER THAN US!
WE'RE IN! LET'S GO!
RUN! HURRY! GET GOING!
RUN TO THE POD! WE CAN MAKE IT. I *KNOW* WE CAN!

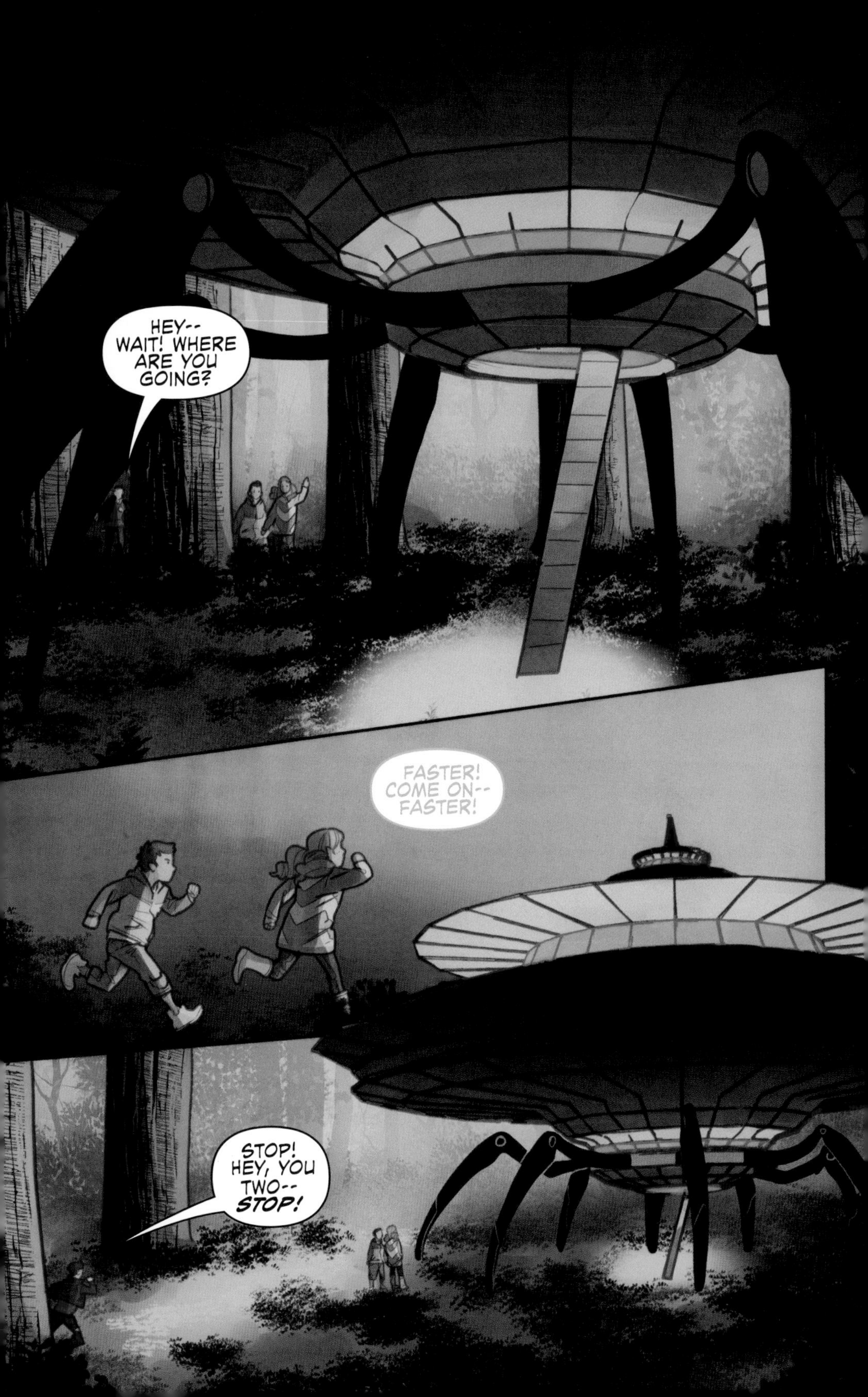
HEY-- WAIT! WHERE ARE YOU GOING?
FASTER! COME ON-- FASTER!
STOP! HEY, YOU TWO-- STOP!

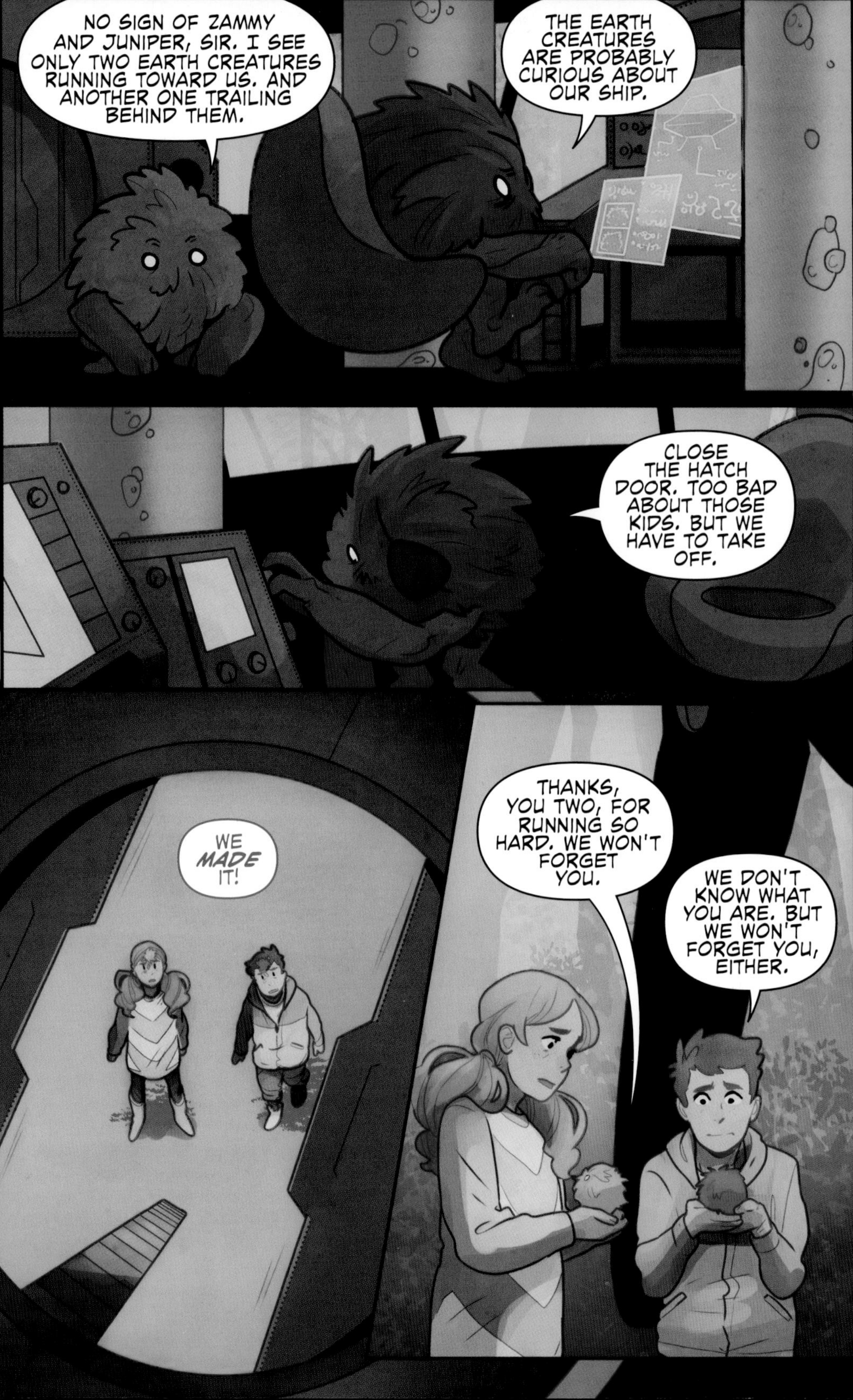
NO SIGN OF ZAMMY AND JUNIPER, SIR. I SEE ONLY TWO EARTH CREATURES RUNNING TOWARD US. AND ANOTHER ONE TRAILING BEHIND THEM.
THE EARTH CREATURES ARE PROBABLY CURIOUS ABOUT OUR SHIP.
CLOSE THE HATCH DOOR. TOO BAD ABOUT THOSE KIDS. BUT WE HAVE TO TAKE OFF.
WE *MADE* IT!
THANKS, YOU TWO, FOR RUNNING SO HARD. WE WON'T FORGET YOU.
WE DON'T KNOW WHAT YOU ARE. BUT WE WON'T FORGET YOU, EITHER.

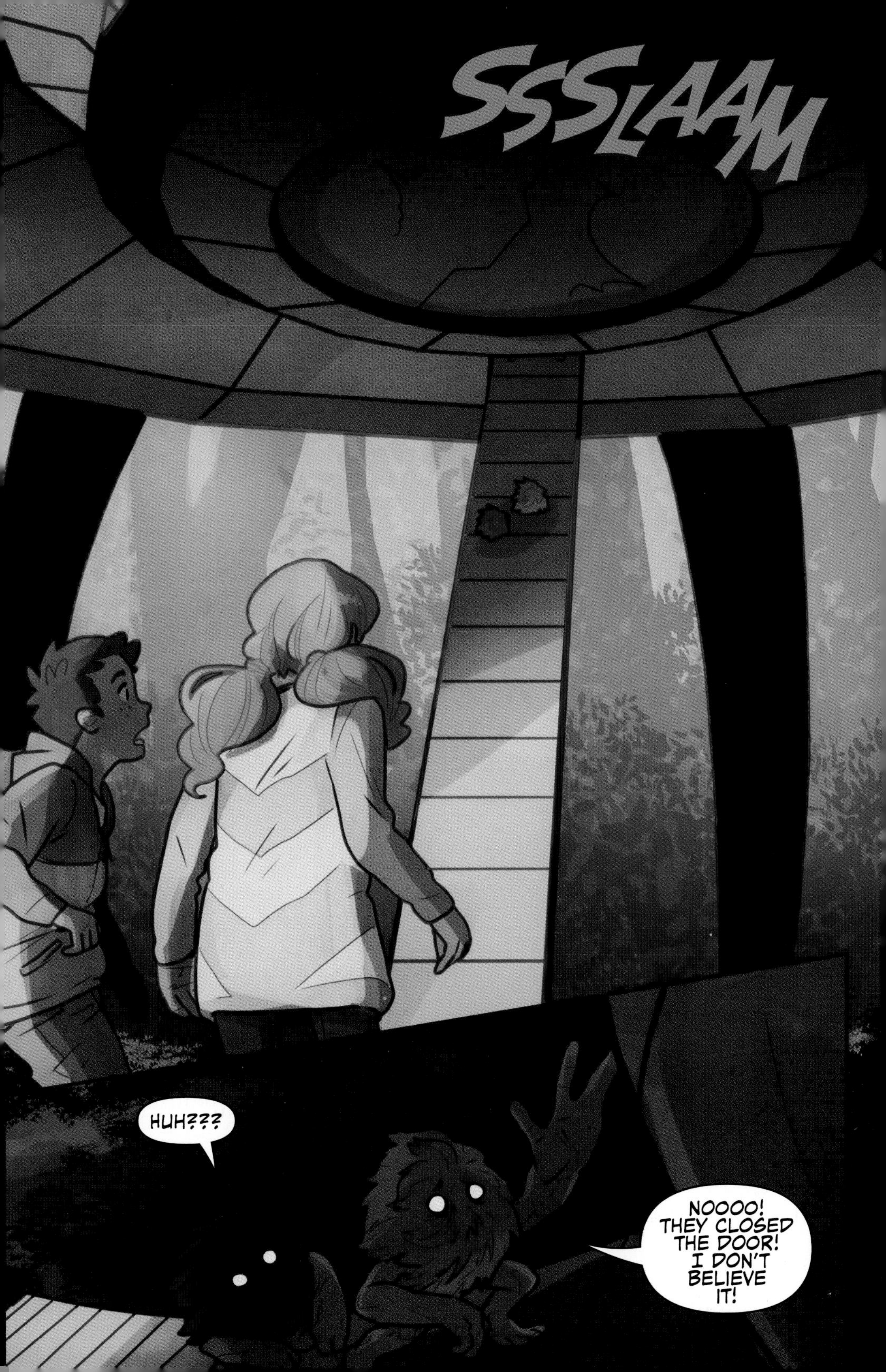
SSSLAAM
HUH???
NOOOO! THEY CLOSED THE DOOR! I DON'T BELIEVE IT!

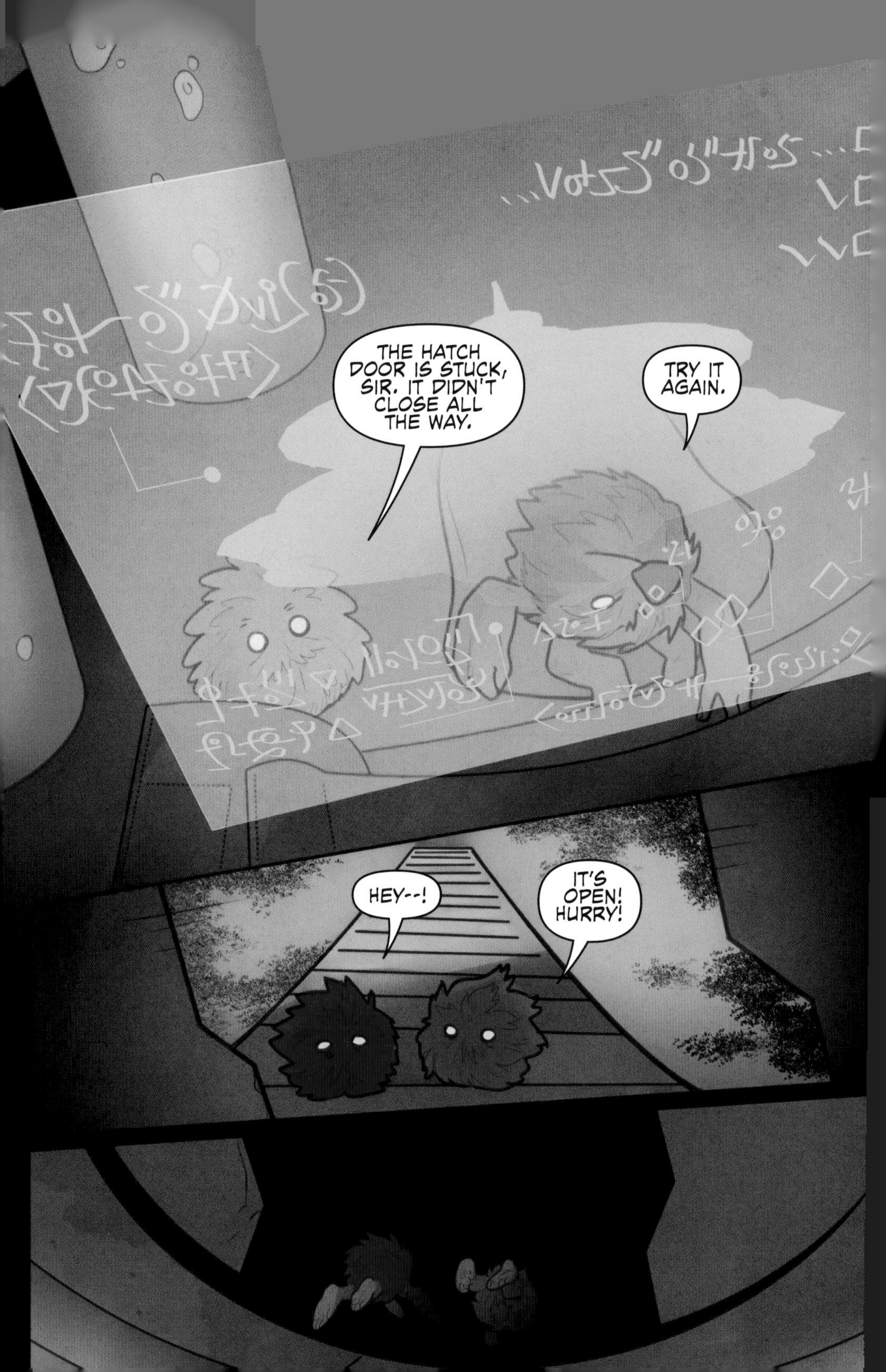
THE HATCH DOOR IS STUCK, SIR. IT DIDN'T CLOSE ALL THE WAY.
TRY IT AGAIN.
HEY--!
IT'S OPEN! HURRY!

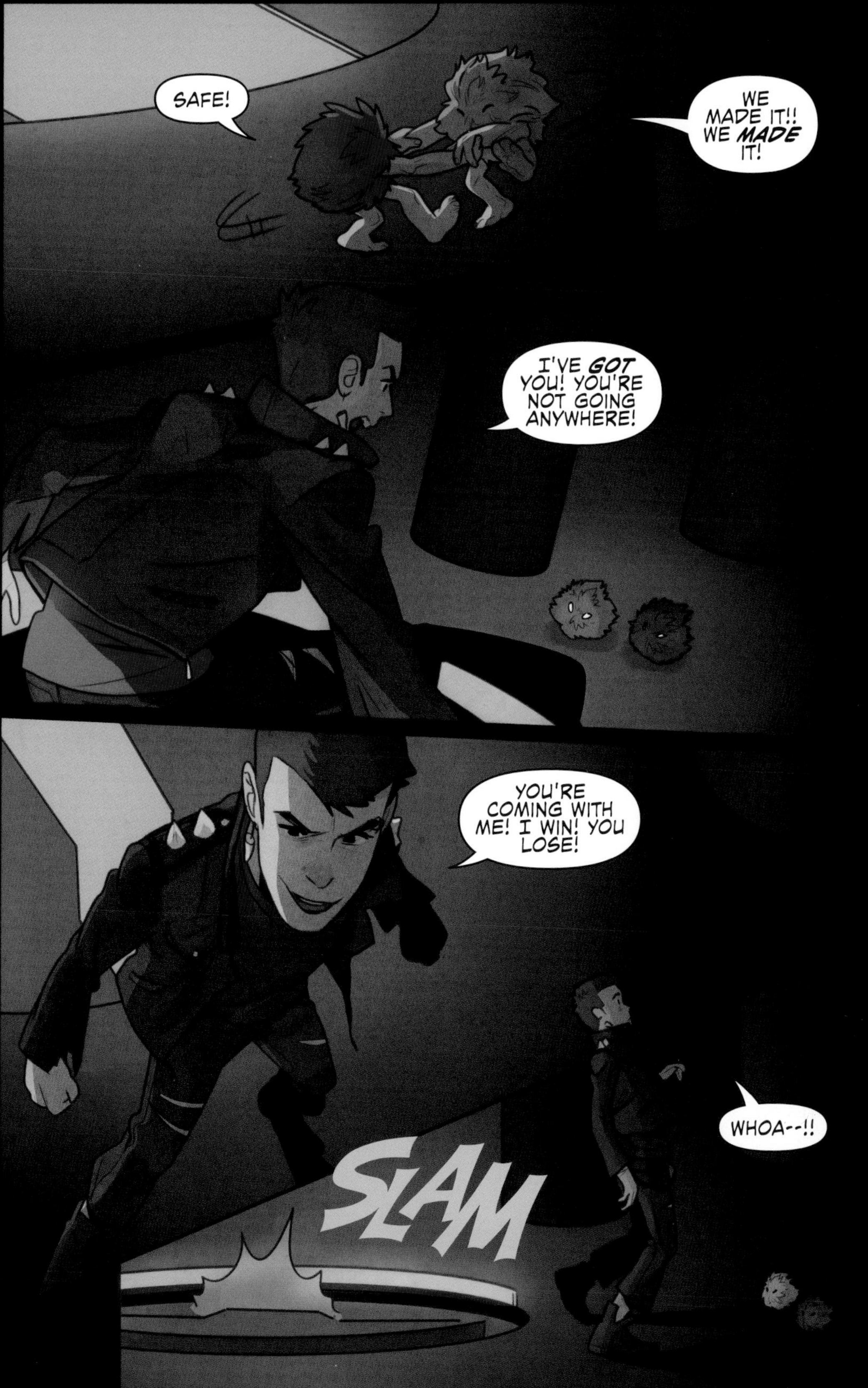
SAFE!
WE MADE IT!! WE *MADE* IT!
I'VE *GOT* YOU! YOU'RE NOT GOING ANYWHERE!
YOU'RE COMING WITH ME! I WIN! YOU LOSE!
WHOA--!!
SLAM

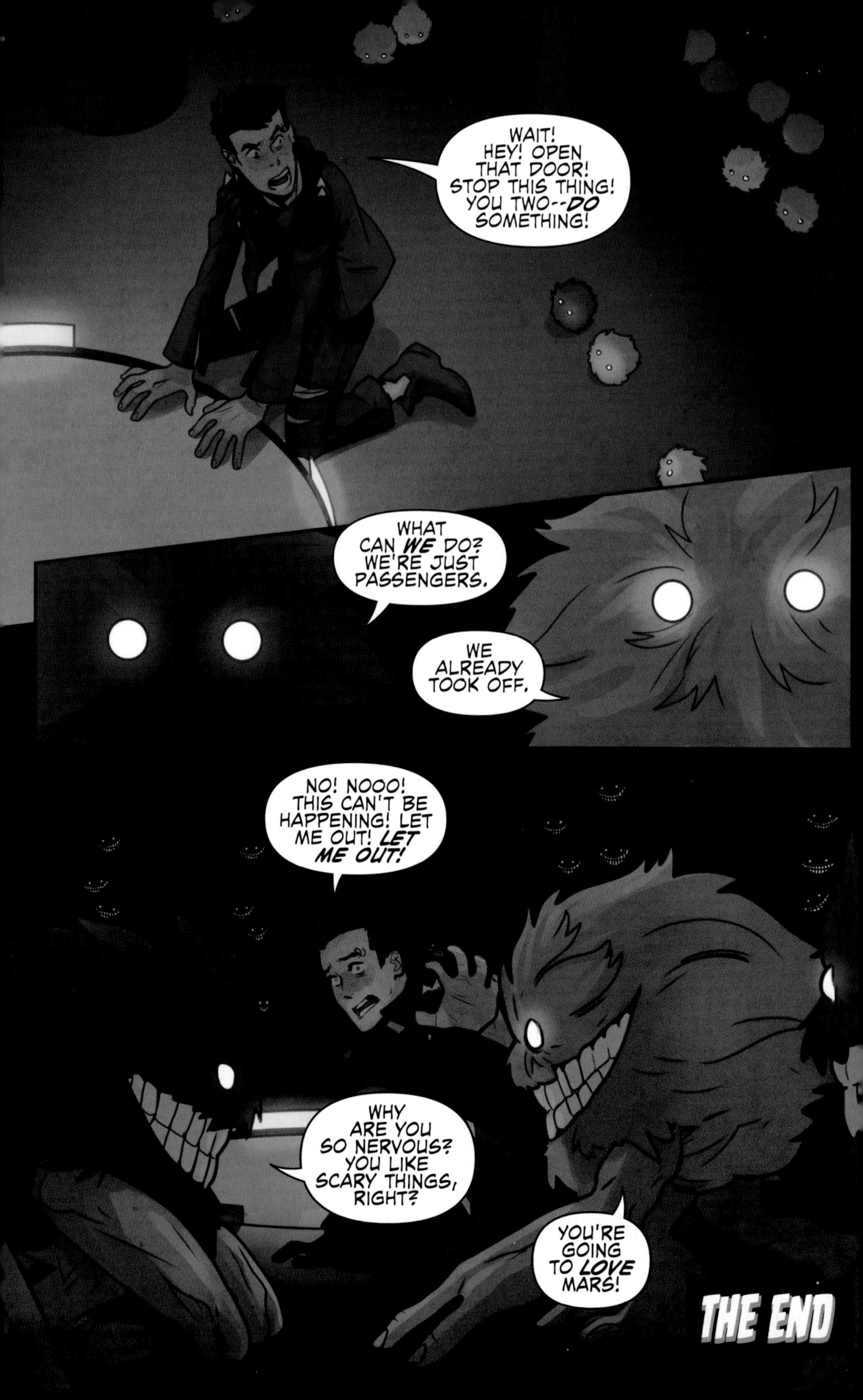
WAIT! HEY! OPEN THAT DOOR! STOP THIS THING! YOU TWO--*DO* SOMETHING!
WHAT CAN *WE* DO? WE'RE JUST PASSENGERS.
WE ALREADY TOOK OFF.
NO! NOOO! THIS CAN'T BE HAPPENING! LET ME OUT! *LET ME OUT!*
WHY ARE YOU SO NERVOUS? YOU LIKE SCARY THINGS, RIGHT?
YOU'RE GOING TO *LOVE* MARS!
THE END